Howell Elvet Lewis

Sweet Singers of Wales

Howell Elvet Lewis

Sweet Singers of Wales

ISBN/EAN: 9783337327590

Printed in Europe, USA, Canada, Australia, Japan

Cover: Foto ©Andreas Hilbeck / pixelio.de

More available books at **www.hansebooks.com**

SWEET SINGERS OF WALES

A Story of

WELSH HYMNS AND THEIR AUTHORS

WITH ORIGINAL TRANSLATIONS

BY

H. ELVET·LEWIS

Dygymydd Duw ag Emyn
Gor. Owain

London

THE RELIGIOUS TRACT SOCIETY

56, PATERNOSTER ROW, 65, ST. PAUL'S CHURCHYARD
AND 164, PICCADILLY

PREFACE.

SEVERAL of these papers appeared in the *Sunday at Home* during 1887-8. They were very kindly received; and as a consequence they have been revised and much enlarged, and are now offered in a separate volume.

No history of Welsh Hymnology has been written in the vernacular. But I must acknowledge my indebtedness, in the historical part, to articles by the Revs. Thomas Rees, D.D., of Swansea; Wm. Rees, D.D., of Liverpool; W. Glanffrwd Thomas, of St. Asaph; and W. Alonzo Griffiths, of Sketty. Especially in the case of Mrs. Ann Griffiths, I owe much to her biography, edited by Mr. Morris Davies. Beside this, I have been aided in several matters by my friends the Revs. J. B. Jones, B.A., Brecon, and J. Evans-Owen, Llanberis.

In the hymns themselves my chief help has come from EMYNAU Y CYSSEGR ('Hymns of the

Sanctuary,') a national collection published by
Messrs. Gee and Son, Denbigh. To them I am also
obliged for permission to use some of the copyright
hymns; and to Messrs. Hughes and Son, Wrexham,
for a similar permission in the case of Islwyn's
hymn.

The metres of the original have been adhered to,
except in very few and trivial instances.

The selections given are representative only:
not exhaustive of authors, and much less so of
hymns. Mr. Gee's collection contains 2,685—and
that by no means drains the stream. A few have
attempted more or less in this work before me:
there is plenty of room for others to come after.
May it be to these what it has been to me—a
lasting pleasure of love!

                                    H. ELVET LEWIS.

CONTENTS.

———◦•———

SWEET SINGERS OF WALES.

CHAPTER I.

INTRODUCTORY.

Their Lord they will praise,
Their language they will keep,
Their land they will lose
Except wild Wales.

So sings an ancient poet of Wales—generally alleged to be Taliesin. On whatever lonesome peak he stood, a companion of clouds and storms and far-off dawns, he heard the prayer, and knew the hope of a nation. Wild Wales is still their home; its ancient speech is still their own. The praise of God has been in the land since early Christian days : it has been often subdued, sometimes almost an exile music, but never quite lost. To-day more than ever the best song of the land is the song of God : and the prophetic words haunt its valleys and hills like an immortal echo—' Their God they will praise.'

2

Where hymnal preludes first entered Welsh
literature, it is not easy to say. There are
remainders still extant which go so far back as
the twelfth century. Naturally, these are tinged
with Catholic sentiment; but for the most part
the tinge is very slight, and scarcely hurts their
delicate simplicity. The following free translation
of a bardic hymn out of the *Black Book of
Caermarthen* will show the character of these
earlier compositions:

In the Name of the Lord,
Be it mine Him to praise,
   Who is great in praises:
Him as Ruler I adore,
For He hath increased the fruit
   Of His charity.

God hath guarded us,
God hath made us,
   God will save us:
God is our Hope,
Worthy and perfect—
   Fair is His destiny.

 We are owned of Him,
Who is in the heights
   King of Trinity:
God was sorely tried,
When He was entering
   Into affliction.

God has come forth,
Though He was prisoned
    In His gentleness :
Sovereign most happy,
He shall make us free
    For the day of doom.

He shall bring us to the feast,
In His mildness
    And His lowliness :
In His Paradise,
Holy shall we dwell
    From sin's penalty.

We have no health
But in His chastisement
    And the five strokes :
Unsparing His grief was,
In human defence,
    When He took our flesh.

Unto God we were lost,
Except for the ransom
    By a blameless decree :
From the blood-stained rood
Came salvation forth
    To the wide universe :
Mighty Shepherd,
Never shall the merit
    Of Christ decay.

Davydd Ddu of Hiraddug, who flourished in the
fifteenth century, produced a metrical version of

the *Officium B. Mariae* and of several psalms.
Whether any of these were brought into the
service of the Welsh Church of that age, or not,
we have no means of discovering. In any case
they could not have touched a nation's heart.
They are correct and refined, but they have no
native warmth. However, before another hundred
years had passed, the nation had a Welsh Bible;
and with the native Bible appeared the firstfruits
of a native hymnody.

If the translations included in this volume have
to any extent reproduced the tone of the original,
scarcely will any one fail to perceive their national
characteristics. They are hymns of the heart,
everywhere touched by a light and pleasant fancy.
From first to last they preserve a general feature of
picturesqueness. Almost every verse is a transcript
from Nature—spiritualized and illuminated. We
walk in a song-land of rocks and mountains; of
valleys and running brooks; of beautiful dawns
struggling into day on mist-covered hills, and calm
sunsets of gold breathing peace on land and sea
after a storm of thunder and lightning and rain;
of long winter nights with every song hushed under
the starless skies, and happy spring mornings when
every leaf is a murmur of resurrection. The
verses which are borne in the hearts of Welshmen
wherever they go, and are sung on Western prairie
or beneath the Southern Cross—they are verses
with a picture of some well-remembered scene
changed into a spiritual idea.

English hymnody has become far more picturesque than it used to be. Some of the most
popular of modern hymns are set round with
pleasant hints of Nature. Verses moving drearily
without any light of fancy have had to give place
to a brighter poesy. This little collection may
not, therefore, be considered out of season.

But it is impossible not to feel that only one half
of the story is given. However characteristically
Welsh the words and sentiments of these hymns
may be, the native melodies to which they have
been wedded are perhaps even more so. The
minor tunes of the Welsh sanctuary are as much
a part of the people's religion as Snowdon is of
the county of Arvon. Strangers have been much
impressed with their sweet melancholy—as if they
had come down through the funerals of the
centuries, and rose heavenward from beneath a
yew-tree. Why they have been so studiously kept
out of English tune-books is a question worth
asking. Possibly the harmony would have to be
modified: otherwise I can see nothing to keep
them out. Some of these melodies have of recent
years been introduced locally, and with agreeable
success.

As to the inner meaning of these hymns, it will
be unfolded in the course of the story. They form
a biography in outline of the devotion of the
Christian Church in Wales from the close of the
sixteenth century. Especially do they reflect the
lights and shades of the National Revival of

the last century. Many of them are born of fire
and storm : they are cries of unknown distress—
the cries of those who awoke 'in the region and
shadow of death,'—and remembered where they
were. But through and above all the pain and
joy, the sorrow and relief, the anxiety and trust of
these hymns, there shines one light with even ray
—the light of the Cross and the Lamb of God.

CHAPTER II.

A LAND without hymn or psalm—such seems to
have been the condition of Wales at the beginning
of the sixteenth century. But the spiritual awakening which resulted in a translation of the whole
Bible into Welsh, turned the mind of contemporary
poets to the study of hymnology. The first edition
of the Welsh Bible was published in 1588; and its
appearance heralded the new era of sacred song.
There were pious patriots who sorrowed much that
while England, Scotland, France, and Italy, had
each its voice of praise in the temple of the
Christian Faith, 'poor little Wales' stood at the
gate, hymnless and forgotten. The first to give
public expression to this sorrow was MAURICE
KYFFIN; of whom very little is known, except his
able translation of Bishop Jewel's *Apologia Ec-
clesiae Anglicanae.* It is in the introduction (dated
London, 1594) to this book that he laments the
absence of song in the church and the home; and
remarks—'Whoever beginneth this sacred labour

must have understanding of several learned languages, so that he give no word in the rhyme but shall be entirely consonant with the mind of the Holy Ghost. Had I the quiet and leisure which many have, the first thing, and the most desirable pain I would take upon me, were to approach this work, after a conference with the learned men of Wales as to what form and what kind of metre would be best and fittest for such piety.' Even while he was writing thus, another religious patriot, in another part of the world, was making leisure for himself to ' begin the sacred labour.'

This was Captain WILLIAM MIDDLETON, who joined to the congenial task of fighting the Spaniards this gentler exercise of translating the Psalms into the language of his beloved motherland, ' keeping as near as he could to the mind of the Holy Ghost.' No doubt the warlike tones of many of these sacred ballads of the Hebrew nation found a ready response in his heart, as he pursued those whom the theology of the day classified as enemies of the Lord. In 1591, six ships were told off under the command of Admiral Howard to go and plunder a portion of the Spanish fleet on its return with large booty from America. Captain Middleton's ship was one of the six, and he was charged to watch the arrival of the enemy. He found, however, that the Spaniards had obtained large reinforcements to defend their treasure, and the mission of plunder had to be abandoned. The captain, we are told, was worthy of a place, even among the brilliant array of brave soldiers that made England's name a terror to the terrible Armada. But in the midst of his naval duties his heart was secretly devoted to a far nobler purpose. He wanted to give his country the Book of Psalms in verse, that the praise of God might no longer be silent. The work was finished at the Island of Scutum, in the West Indies, on the 24th day of January, 1595. But, alas, for good intentions without due regard to practical results! His metres were all so intricate that no music could fit them, and no mouth could sing them. So the book has always remained a pious failure; one of the many fruitless works of well-meaning devotion which lie on the road to heaven, like broken columns of white ·marble, covered with dust—of very little value here, but in heaven surely remembered ' for the Name that is dear.'

While the sailor-poet was finishing his version in the West Indies, another kindred spirit at home—EDWARD KYFFIN, supposed by some to be a brother of Maurice—was preparing some of the Psalms ' for such of his beloved countrymen as love the glory of the Lord and the cherishing of their own mother tongue.' In his introduction he is careful to explain, with a touch of true Elizabethan ' sea-divinity,' that Englishmen were not only zealous to rob and kill the Spaniards, but had also an anxious desire to save their souls ; for had they not printed a large number of religious books in Spanish, and distributed them very diligently—when not otherwise engaged? If a foreign nation merited so much Christian consideration, how much more his own nation? for assuredly no people had been so favoured of God for long centuries, and were they to be last and latest in speaking of His glory?

He only versified thirteen Psalms; but he prays most earnestly that this may be an incitement to some other mind to finish the work: 'hoping that since God has kept us so long, He may have in His thought some *chef d'œuvre* and mighty conquest for the increase of His own glory among the ancient Britons, whom He has so miraculously preserved until now in liberty and safety.' The introduction breathes throughout a spirit of exalted devotion: and after three hundred years every sentence seems as if the touch of Heaven were fresh upon it. ' Let no true Welshman give sleep to his eyes or slumber to his eyelids, as the prophet David said, until he has seen the glory of the Lord, by facilitating the completion of this godly task in the language of his own country!"

His appeal was not in vain. EDMUND PRYS, before twenty years had passed, published a complete Welsh Psalter. He was an Archdeacon of Merioneth, a man of scholarly attainments, and an eminent poet. Born, about 1541, in the romantic neighbourhood of Harlech, the fellowship of Nature in the charming ruggedness of hill and glen, and in the shining blue of the sea, would establish a community of thought, and of sacred fancy between him and the poet-king of Israel, who read the signature of the Divine hand on every page of creation. I am afraid, nevertheless, that this poetic genius was sometimes scarcely under control. Among all the bardic quarrels of Welsh literature, his quarrel with William Cynwal must be counted as its Iliad. The latter was a smith by trade, and received one day a message in verse from the archdeacon, asking for a steel bow to be sent to a friend, according to promise. The smith—who was also a poet—made a long delay, and sent his excuses back in verse. So the battle began and went on, poem for poem; till the archdeacon began to treble his blows, sending three satires together, and receiving the same number of fiery missiles' in return. The archdeacon then thought he would finish his adversary with a fusillade of nine poems, but the sturdy blacksmith was sufficiently alive still to reply with another nine. Three times nine poems was the next intended onslaught, but when the archdeacon had finished sixteen of them, a messenger brought him tidings that his rival had reached the dark and silent land where 'there is no work, nor device, nor knowledge, nor wisdom'—nor any noise of warfare! He threw his sword far into the sea, and there and then commenced an elegy bewailing the loss of so brave a foe, so skilful a poet!

So much for the archdeacon's celebrated fight, in which he laboured hard and gained nothing. More profitable is it to chronicle that he found a

new mission in the work mapped out by Maurice
Kyffin, and already initiated by Edward Kyffin.
In turning the whole of the Psalms into verse—
and verse that could be sung—he has given all
coming ages cause to bless the regeneration of his
muse.

It is said that his custom was to prepare a
Psalm for each Sunday, to be chanted in the
church. His intimate knowledge of Hebrew
helped him to give sometimes a better rendering
of the original than that even in the Authorized
Version of the Welsh Bible. The whole was
published in 1621. While the version has suffered
somewhat from a lack of variety in its metre, it
has nevertheless been, ever since its first appearance, one of the chief treasures of Welsh
hymnology. Many a single verse, rugged and
massive of form, has done yeoman service on 'the
field of Association' (maes y Gymanfa); when, as
in the earlier part of the present century, it was
uttered by the lips of a John Elias, and taken up
by the large assembly in unison, at first in slow
and halting tones, gradually rising and swelling,
till at last with overwhelming force it seemed to
break on the shore of ten thousand souls like
the splendid rush and roar of a mighty sea. On
occasions like this, a favourite verse of that famous
preacher was the archdeacon's rendering of Psalm
lvii. 11 : 'Be Thou exalted, O God, above the
heavens : let Thy glory be above all the earth.'
And another—equally appropriate before speaking

the eternal word to the great assembly—was the rendering of Psalm cxli. 3 : ' Set a watch, O Lord, before my mouth ; keep the door of my lips.' How effective such a verse, spoken by such a man in such a place, might be, let the following graphic description of him bear witness—drawn by Gwalchmai, a living poet and preacher :

' Mr. Elias rises up to the desk. He casts a glance over all the congregation. He requests those who stand on the edge of the crowd to close in toward the centre. The sight of him is very striking; his whole aspect is winning; there is a noble dignity in his look ; greatness is interwoven with humility in his personal appearance. He comes forward as a general to lead an army—a captain of the host of the Lord ; or rather as an ambassador for his King. No one asks to see his seals of office : every one reads his authority in his appearance. . . . His thought fills every line, every muscle, every vein in his face. Sparks of fire leap out of his eyes, and still at the same time the most diffident tenderness clothes his countenance. He looks as anxious as if this were to be the last association in which he would ever appear publicly to deliver his message for his great Master ; he seems as if he thought that he is on the point of being summoned to render an account to his King ; and on that account he commands every feeling, every nerve, every faculty, and every purpose he possesses, to his important and solemn task. He is as if he wanted to make one immortal exploit.

To-day or never, to save the souls in his presence !
He gives out a verse to sing, with a sonorousness
like that of a golden bell in his mouth :

> " Set on my mouth a seal, O Lord,
> Lest witty word offendeth ;
> Cover my lips, lest I speak ill
> What now Thy will me sendeth." '

The severe, rugged strength of the words in the
Welsh original moves like a torrent in its course ;
and the preacher used the mighty and awful words
to bring himself into the current of Divine
eloquence. No wonder that, with 'the door' of
God upon his lips, his sermon was as the visible
fire of heaven.

The above gives some hint of the place taken by
the archdeacon's Psalter in the national history.
Perhaps a still clearer glimpse of its power is
afforded by this memorable incident connected with
the singing of his version of Psalm cxxi. 1, 2.

One of the evangelist preachers of the eighteenth
century ventured to cross over to Anglesey to publish the glad tidings of God. His appearance was
the signal for violent opposition ; and how it fared
with him on one occasion shall be told in the words
of one who ought to know :

' Saul of Tarsus was never more determined to
imprison the disciples of Jesus than I, and the
persecuting band that had gathered together with
staves to meet the Roundhead who was coming to

preach at Penmynydd. We had all agreed, if he tried to preach, to make an end of him there and then. When he had arrived, we began to push forwards close to him; and when he had mounted a large stone which stood beside the house, and turned his face toward Carnarvon, and gave out this stanza, to be sung by his scanty followers:

" I lift mine eyes unto the hills
Whence willing help shall come,"

we, supposing him to be expecting some armed men from the hills of Arvon, began to retreat a little. And after consultation, some of us decided to hear what the preacher had to say; and so we went over the fence, and crept slowly and noise-lessly under cover of it till we came over against where he stood. He could not see us, and we did not want to see him; but we could hear every word he said as plainly as if we stood beside him. Under that sermon, on the most wonderful day of my life, I came to know myself as a lost sinner —lost everywhere, and in everything, outside of Jesus Christ, and Him crucified.'

A century passed away from the death of Edmund Prys before Providence in its own strange way found another sacred poet; this time in the person of a cattle-dealer. DAVID JONES, of Cayo, Caermarthenshire, was accustomed to buy cattle from the fairs about his home, and take them over to Barnet and Maidstone to sell. He had received a fair education in his youth, and being quick-witted and sociable, he soon obtained a considerable command of the English language ; and so he must have been a *rara avis* in his native district, when 'no English' was the order of the day. During his travels he picked up many a marvellous tale and choice bit of gossip: this made him a charming and valued guest in the country inns far and near. His ready verse also was 'violin and harp' for merry comrades during the long evenings of winter; or even on the Sabbath day when some festival of devilry was to be held, as was not unfrequently the case. But an unexpected change came over him—came in a simple but wondrous fashion. One Sunday morning, when he was returning from an expedition into England, he caught the sound of singing in the old Independent chapel of Troedrhiwdalar, Brecon-shire, and was attracted thereby to enter. A message from God was there for him that morning. He left the chapel with the old life of vanity and sin for ever judged ; and before him rose the hope of Jesus Christ, like a summer dawn on the hills which sheltered his Vale of Towy. His heart once changed, his poetic talents were soon touched by the fire from the seraph's hand. The minstrel of the public-house became the sweet singer of Zion. The religion of the day was becoming so profoundly Christ-conscious, that the classical Psalter of Archdeacon Prys was inadequate to express its emotion. But the evangelical Psalter of Dr. Watts had in England largely satisfied this religious fervency. So David Jones gave himself with eager sympathy to the work of translating Dr. Watts' Psalms and Hymns; and in this he achieved decided success.

Many of his verses remain the most popular and homely of all versions of Israel's national songs, and are household treasures of Welsh piety. But he was not satisfied with merely doing the work of a translator: he composed several hymns of permanent merit, touched with the spirit of the Great Revival of the eighteenth century. It was the day when the living gospel had to be preached in some humble cottage or on the public street. Once, when a service was being held near Lampeter, where David Jones had gone, according to his wont, to accompany the evangelist, a band of hired ruffians set on the house and dragged the worshippers out to the street with great violence. There the poet knelt down on the ground, and began to pray. He was a man of prayer; and in that hour of trial every word seemed to find the Almighty God. The persecutors stood still; they were startled; they became terrified. Without waiting further they escaped for their lives, lest they should be smitten by the God of the man who prayed in the street.

It was the day of religious ecstasy. He himself used to break out sometimes into exalted expressions of religious fervour, praising God aloud in the assembly, and 'laughing tears' in the vision of Divine Love. Belonging, as he did, to the

3

'dry Dissenters'—a term of contempt applied to
the quieter religionists of the day—he was sometimes called to task by his brethren for what they
considered his extravagance. His reply to all such
accusations is given in some characteristic verses,
of which the following is a free translation :

Men of the world are asking,
　Much wondering at me,
When I my Lord am praising,
　'What can this folly be ?'
I am released from bondage,
　And though the mockers throng,
The precious blood of Jesus
　Shall always be my song.

A cloud once darkened o'er me,
　No praises could I sing ;
Sin and its guilty sorrow
　Pierced through me with its sting :
But that has been removèd,
　And all its weight of pain—
The precious blood of Jesus
　I sing, and sing again.

I stood at Sinai trembling,
　Where God upon me frowned ;
Dark threatenings broke in thunders,
　The lightning flashed around :
I came to peaceful Zion—
　How can I songless be ?—
The precious blood of Jesus
　all the world to me.

What, though I leap rejoicing ?
Sweet reverence guides my thought ;
Like David's godly dancing
When home the ark was brought ;
Or, like the lame man's rapture,
Healed at the temple gate—
The precious blood of Jesus
Brought health and good estate.

Another simple and earnest hymn of his is the following :

Come, brethren, unite
In holy delight,
To praise our Belovèd—redemption's great Light :
How sweet is the care·
His love to declare—
That He should our chastisement faithfully bear.

Great God upon high,
The Lord from the sky,
He came as a Lamb without blemish, to die !
While under the sun,
Our duty is one—
To publish the merits and gifts of the Son.

A poor man He came,
Enduring our shame,
To be our Redeemer—our Brother by name :
Declare His renown,
The rights of His crown—
His life for the sheep hath the Shepherd laid down !

His blood hath made peace,
And brought us release ;
And now the old bondage for ever must cease :
Who trust in His might
He leads into light ;
Nor can any enemy break on His right.

CHAPTER III.

WILLIAM WILLIAMS, PANTYCELYN.

What Paul Gerhardt has been to Germany, what Isaac Watts has been to England, that and more has William Williams, of Pantycelyn, been to the little principality of Wales. His hymns have both stirred and soothed a whole nation for more than a hundred years : they have helped to fashion a nation's character and to deepen a nation's piety. They have been sung by the shepherd on the moor and on the mountain, in the midst of romantic solitudes; or by the smith to the accompaniment of his ringing anvil; or by the miner in the weird halls of buried forests underneath the ground ; or by the milkmaid, with a fresh, clear voice, as she brushed from the clover the dewdrops of an early morning in May; or by the reaper in the harvest-field as he gathered in the golden grain.

The mother hums one of his tender musings above the cradle of her child, surrounding its soft-winged slumbers with the praises of Him whose 'very name is music.' The funeral procession takes up one of his strains of sorrow touched with hope, and sings it when accompanying the dead to the long home—sings it musingly, measuredly,

moaningly. The young man in the day of trial
will take some smooth stones out of this brook
of Christian poetry, and with them overcome the
enemy. The veteran soldier of God thirsts for the
water out of this 'well of Bethlehem,' and 'pours
it out before the Lord.' Through some memorial
verse of his the family of the Lord Christ has often
expressed its sweet sorrowfulness of heart, as it
looked on the breaking of the bread. Many a time
has the sad Angel of Death heard one of his
victorious strains fall from some trusting soul as it
passed through the dark gateway—heard the echo
of the song far down in the Valley of the Shadow:
a strange thing of joy: like a warm sunbeam
piercing through the chill eternal twilight of some
ancient forest of pine. It was a verse of his that
Christmas Evans—one of the immortal 'three' of
the Welsh pulpit—sang when nearing home; taking
it as a staff in his hand, 'and smiting Jordan
with it, so that the waters were divided hither and
thither, and he went over on dry ground ':

> O Thou Righteousness eternal!
> Righteousness of boundless store!
> Soon my naked, hungry spirit
> Must enjoy Thee evermore :
> Hide my nakedness, oh ! hide it,
> With Thy robe of shining white;
> So that, fearless, I may ever
> Stand before Thy throne of light.

Like all poets that have deeply stirred a people,

he was brought up in troublous times. His father was the deacon of a famous Independent church in Caermarthenshire, which had to meet for a time in a cave during the hours of twilight, on account of the persecution to which a large number of the sincerest Christians of the age were subjected. But when the poet was very young he lost his father, and was left to the care of his mother. He spent some years at college, purposing to devote himself to the medical profession. It was on his way home from college that an incident happened which changed his whole career. He was passing through the little village of Talgarth, in Breconshire, on a Sunday morning, when he was attracted by the sound of a bell to enter the parish church. The service was cold and spiritless, and left scarcely any impression whatever on the young man's mind.

The people on leaving church, instead of scattering and wending their way home, grouped themselves together in the churchyard, and every face was alive with expectation, as though eagerly waiting for something more. And more did come. It affords a striking picture of the religious life of Wales near the middle of the eighteenth century. On one of the gravestones a man of short stature and exceedingly sombre face takes his stand. In a moment every eye is fastened upon him in a solemn, nervous suspense. Then the voice begins to ring deep and clear and earnest among the grey tombstones—like the voice of some ancient prophet of Israel summoning the people with words of fire to repent forthwith and escape for their life. The congregation is stirred, startled, confounded : it moves to and fro, 'as the trees of the wood are moved by the wind.' Strong men are there, weeping like little children, terrible to see ; while others in their rage against the preacher curse like a demoniac at the approach of the Lord Christ. Here a woman falls fainting: another cries out through a storm of sobs and tears, ' What must we do ? ' And the young poet ? ' There he is, his face deathly pale, and his whole body shaken with excitement and terror. He is a very image of fearfulness. He stands each moment expecting to see the Son of Man coming on the clouds of heaven : a sharp, glowing arrow from the bow of the doctrine of the man on the gravestone has pierced through his heart.' He came out of that historic churchyard with the light of eternity in his eyes.

Two or three years afterwards he was ordained deacon of the Church of England. But in those days the Church of England was her own unrelenting enemy in Wales. Like many another of her servants of best worth, he was excommunicated on an indictment of committing twenty-four crimes—chief among them being his refusal to make the sign of the cross in baptism, and his zeal in preaching the gospel outside of places properly consecrated. He had come under the influence of Whitefield, who urged him to go forth to the highways to proclaim the glad tidings. And preach he did from Holyhead to Cardiff, having travelled on an average 3,000 miles every year for fifty years.

As a preacher, he was a son of consolation. His sermons, like his hymns, were expressions of profound experience—the sorrow and joy of a pilgrim who had travelled for a long time heavy-laden, and at last had ' his burden loosed from off his shoulders ' at the place where ' stood a cross, and a little below, in the bottom, a sepulchre.' He was a poet in the pulpit, with all a poet's swift change of feeling. In a conversation with his co-worker, the Rev. Peter Williams—well known in Wales still for his annotated Bible—he remarked, with his usual quaint humour : ' As for thee, Peter, thou couldest get through it well enough if the Holy Spirit were in America ; but I can make nothing of it unless He is near.'

Williams first exercised his gift of sacred song at an association held in the earliest days of Welsh Calvinistic Methodism. The hymns hitherto used were foreign to the spirit of the new movement ; but as soon as he began to pour forth his varied strains of passionate sweetness, Howell Harris, the preacher of Talgarth Churchyard, pronounced him a master of song. His hymns seemed to fly abroad as on the wings of the wind, and soon became the sacred ballads of the whole nation. As Luther sang Germany into Protestantism, so did Williams sing the Wales of the eighteenth century into piety.

His hymns are full of pictures from Nature. It
could be almost said that the natural aspects of his
native land through all the changes of the twelve
months are reflected and reproduced in his hymns.
The heavy clouds of storm, and the white clouds of
a summer day—clouds gathering with dark fore-
bodings on the horizon, clouds beautifully passing
away at eventide after a rainy day—clouds of
thunder with fringes of chilly white, and the fleet-
ing clouds of April: they are all here. He has
watched the dawn deepening in the east, he has
walked in the glow of noon, he has looked with
sobering eye on the sunset glories of the west. He
has wandered beside the mountain brook and the
calm river, and he has seen the brown torrents
raging on the hillsides. He knows the charm of a
spring day after a long winter; and the sweet
pensiveness of yellow corn-fields and tinted autumn
leaves. He has found quiet havens of the sea, and
felt the joy of the morning star rising above the
waves. Some of these pictures will appear in the
hymns reproduced here: but to reproduce all his
etchings from Nature would be to give almost all
his hymns.

Once, during a long season of drought, he was
walking through the fields, and found some little
beasts of prey making busy mischief among the
green corn; whereon he pertinently asked:

Why should beasts of prey be suffered
To destroy the tender blade?

Why should sweet and youthful blossoms
  In the drought be left to fade?
Bring the pleasant showers refreshing,
  That the grain may flourish soon;
Bring a shower the early morning,
  Bring one more the afternoon.

Jesus, turn the living rivers
  O'er the dry and rocky land;
So make beautiful the corn-fields
  With the blessings of Thy hand;
From the cool and crystal fountain
  Give to him who fainting lies;
Who has toiled without a shelter
  All the day 'neath burning skies.

On another occasion he was staying for the night not far from the Prescelly Hills. Being up early next morning, he saw the whole range lying dark and frowning under the mist; but in the east the dawn was breaking up the shadows of night, and the sky was brightening with the promise of a new day—a picture which he has introduced into his well-known missionary hymn—

O'er the gloomy hills of darkness.

This, and 'Guide me, O Thou great Jehovah,' are the only two translated hymns of his that have found favour with editors of English hymnals. I believe the missionary hymn was written originally in English, and translated by his son into Welsh. The other is found in a little volume of English hymns he published under the title of *Gloria in Excelsis*, for use in Mr. Whitefield's Orphans' House in America. It was prepared at the request of Lady Huntingdon, who had been much impressed by some other writings of his. Mr. Whitefield included it in his collection of hymns published in 1774; and since then it has had a place in most hymnals.

He suffered sometimes from absent-mindedness, as the following tradition indicates. He was one day far away from home, holding a service beside the sea-shore. A friend had taken the devotional portion of the service, when, as he drew near the close of his prayer, a cuckoo began to sing. Williams stood up to give out a hymn before preaching: it was an appeal to the cuckoo to fly away to Pantycelyn and tell 'Mally' his wife that he was alive; to proceed from thence to Builth and tell 'Jack' his son to 'keep his place'; concluding with the pious wish that should they fail to meet again on earth, they might meet in heaven. His friend touched him and hinted that the doctrine of salvation was rather scanty in his verse. 'Very true,' replied the poet at once; and, without any more ado, gave out another verse, which seems to carry in it everywhere the sound of the everlasting sea—the music of an infinite hope for man:

> Salvation like a boundless sea
>   Keeps swelling on the shore;
> Here shall the weak and helpless find
>   Enough for evermore.

Another instance of his ready wit was recently given by a South Wales correspondent.[1] It seems that he was at Aberdare one day preaching from the text—'The harvest truly is great, but the labourers are few ; pray ye, therefore, the Lord of the harvest that He would send forth labourers into His harvest.' After the sermon he gave out a hymn in a metre which was not known to any of the masters of song present. Apprehending their difficulty, he immediately put them right again by giving out an extempore verse, of which the following is a translation :

> To-day are ye not saying—
> 'Four months will come and go,
> And then with fruitful harvest
> The fields will be aglow':
> But saith the King of heaven—
> 'Lift up your eyes around!'
> White are the fields already
> Where His good wheat is found.

So much for tales of eccentric origins; which prove, besides, how lively a sympathy existed between the poet's mind and the varying phases of Nature. In further illustration of this, the following group of four hymns is given; showing successive reflections of a summer evening, a winter's night, a clear morning after a stormy night, and a calm sea after contrary winds.

In the first hymn we seem to be gazing on the

[1] ' Cosmos ' in *The South Wales Daily News.*

sunset sky of a peaceful summer evening ; and the
heavenly quiet of the scene awakens in the soul
infinite longings that are sad in their very sweetness :

> I look beyond the far-off hills,
>   O gentle Christ, for Thee :
> Come, my Belovèd, it is late,
>   The sun goes down on me.

> These captive weeks of Babylon
>   Make sorrow long delay :
> Oh ! that I heard the jubilee
>   Opening the gates of day.

> If from these fetters hard and cold
>   My feet were only free,
> Long as I lived I would but sing
>   The grace of Calvary.

> A pilgrim in a desert land
>   I wander far and near,
> Expecting every hour to find
>   My Father's house appear.

Next comes this winter-night's hymn :

> While the stormy winds are blowing
>   From the north so bleak and chill,
> Saviour, keep my soul defended
>   From the fear of coming ill :
>   Change the winter
>   Into balmy days and still.

Oh ! that now the world would leave me,
  Oh ! that now the skies would clear,
And the land of pleasant ranges
  O'er the distant hills appear !
      Then my spirit
  Would be calm with holy cheer.

But the strength of passion paineth,
  And I feel my guilt unspent,
While I cannot cease from sinning—
  Failing even to repent :
      Light of sunrise,
  Break this long imprisonment !

Waiting through the long night-watches,
  Waiting for the break of day ;
Waiting for the gates to open,
  And my chains to fall away :
      All in darkness,
  For the light of God I pray.

And my soul shall keep on trusting,
  Looking every day for Thee ;
For Thy hand can save the weakest,
  Yea, the weakest—even me !
      I must tarry
  Till the blessed Jubilee.

Dawn at last ! the dawn is coming,
  And the clouds shall pass away ;
In the valleys, on the mountains,
  Shall the mist no longer stay :
      Hours of heaven,
  Long I waited—now 'tis day.

The last verse is the victory of faith over Nature : the world continues dark outside; but the dayspring from on high has visited the soul. In the next hymn, Faith and Nature stand side by side in the morning light.

The cloud has almost cleared,
That filled me with unrest ;
The northwind too has veered
A little to the west :
After the storm there comes to-day
Fair weather on the heavenly way.

Dark night tempestuous
Will very soon be gone ;
Long ages of the cross
Have been ordained for none :
The dawnlight in the eastern sky
Tells of a glorious morning nigh.

The sun is on the hills
Around my Father's house ;
And through these earthly ills
The light eternal grows :
My hope is sure : who can efface
My name in God's own book of grace ?

Upon His word I rest,
Come all things contrary ;
When in the night distressed
My safe stronghold is He :
Nearer with each return of sun
The promise comes. It shall be done.

But it is neither winter night nor summer eve that has touched the poet's mind in this last hymn of the group. It may have come to him partly through reading the experiences of Columbus when in search of a new continent.

Here I know myself a stranger,
    And my native country lies
Far beyond the ocean's danger,
    In the lands of Paradise:
Storms of trial blowing keenly
    Drove me on this foreign strand;
Come, O South-wind, blow serenely,
    Speed me to my Fatherland.

Though the voyage should be stormy,
    Though the raging billows foam;
Even were the worst before me,
    I shall sometime be at home:
Waves and seas are strong; but stronger
    Is the word of God than all;
Trusting Him I fear no longer,
    Safely in His hands I fall.

Now the air is full of balm
    With the fragrance of the land;
And the breezes clear and calm
    Tell of Paradise at hand:
Come, ye much-desired regions,
    With the best of joy in store:
Country of the singing legions,
    Let me reach thy restful shore!

Williams possessed to a considerable extent the

Shakspearean faculty of seeing many aspects of
human nature, especially on its religious side.
His hymns give expression to every grade of
experience, from the lowest deep of despair to the
clearest height of full assurance.   It is himself
speaking; but in his voice we hear the sobs and
cries, the joys and transports of a thousand hearts.
He gives us a view of his early struggles and
defeats : how seven times back and fore he broke
the commandments of God, and attempted to confirm his deliverance with ' seven great vows ' : but
all in vain, until he saw from the depths the Face
that is ' altogether lovely,' and driven by a flame
of guilt he came to the pleasant hill of Zion: he
had found heaven on the brink of hell, in the
thunders of Sinai he had his first meeting with
God—hours never to be forgotten, the hours of his
marriage with heaven.   But though the violence
of the early conflict is smoothed down, he has not
yet come to the possession of perfect peace :

Once again my sigh of sorrow
  Riseth to His gracious ears ;
For His pity, for His presence,
  Weeps my soul these flowing tears.

Who can tell but He who founded
  Earth and heaven shall hear my cry,
And that all these mournful longings
  God Himself shall satisfy ?

Oh ! to hear the silver trumpet
Now proclaim my full release,
That my heavy-laden spirit
May at last have joy and peace.

Oh ! that now like mighty torrents
Strength descended from above !
Not the strongest of my passions
Could withstand His conquering love.

In another hymn we see him a solitary wanderer
on the high and dangerous mountain footpath ;
the path is very narrow, and underneath him is a
fearful depth. What if he miss his footing !

In Thy hand I cannot fall,
Though the weakest of them all ;
In Thy hand at length I come
From my trials safely home.

He had promised to himself in the morning to
be at home early, having overcome all his enemies
—but 'the noise of battle is yet in the country
where I live.' He is sometimes afraid even that
he has not yet received 'officacious grace,' and
that his sins may yet win the day. What can he
do but pray God to lift him out of the pit ? And
even if it is growing late, he must wait until 'the
Morning Star rise over yonder hills.' His trial,
too, had bound him in sweet fellowship with all
who strive upward to God :

Much I love the faithful pilgrims,
  Who the rugged steeps ascend;
On their hands and knees they labour
  To attain the heavenly end:
    To the summit
  On my knees shall I come too.

Bruisèd hands, oh! stretch ye upward,
  Tired feet, walk ye with care;
The reward, the crown is yonder,
  My Belovèd—He is there!
    Earth forsaking;
  Now the journey's end is all.

In the company of the same singer, what a
burst of triumphant faith we have in this martial
strain:

The standard is ahead,
  The gospel of His grace;
And hell is filled with dread,
  And shakes before His face:
Down! down! with shame it shall be brought,
Before my Jesus it is nought.

Great hosts from prisons free
  Already have marched on,
And great their joy must be
  To know the day is won:
From strife and toil on high they fled,
And in their footsteps we must tread.

Leave we the world behind,
  The world that made us smart,
The world, of evil mind
  Each day to break our heart :
Between the stars behold the light
Of that far better world in sight !

The blood of Jesu's cross
  Was never shed in vain ;
There is not any loss
  Of His most precious pain :
This is the great, the finished plan
To open heaven's door for man.

Let all bow down and own
  The sacrificèd Lamb !
Among all titles known
  His is the greatest name :
Praise, laud, and blessing to our Lord,
Let Him be evermore adored !

Side by side with this call of Christian soldiers
to battle we may place a hymn to the Lord of
Battles, the Captain of the Christian host.

Ride to battle, ride victorious,
  Gird, O Christ, Thy glittering sword ;
Earth can never stand before Thee,
  Nor can hell itself, my Lord :
In Thy name such glory dwelleth,
  Hostile armies faint with fear ;
And the wide creation trembleth
  When it feels Thee coming near.

Now release my soul from bondage,
　Let the heavenly day be known :
Burst the iron bars in sunder,
　Raze the gates of Babylon :
Thrust the captives hence in armies,
　Like the torrents of a flood ;
Thousand after thousand singing,
　Countless—ransomed—multitude !

Even now methinks I hear them,
　Voices singing from afar ;
They extol the great redemption,
　In the land where freemen are :
All of them have snow-white garments,
　And aloft the palms they bear ;
Crowned with glory all-abounding
　Into life they enter there.

Be it mine to share the gladness
　Of that joyful day of days ;
Every word that Christ has spoken
　Shall fulfil itself in grace :
North and south—ten times ten thousand,
　From the night that covered them,
Come with sound of silver trumpets
　To the New Jerusalem.

The Christ of the glittering sword and the
glorious terror—can He speak to the broken heart
and bring glad tidings to the frightened conscience ?
Yes, verily :

Speak, O Christ! the gentle-hearted,
　For Thy words are God's best wine ;
All within me peace creating,
　Peace of endless worth divine ;

All the voices of creation,
 Every passion and delight,
At Thy voice of quiet sweetness,
 Pass away in hushed affright.

This world's empty noises vanish
 When Thou speakest but a word;
And the tumult is dispersèd,
 By opposing passions stirred;
Though the afternoon was stormy,
 Cloudless is the evening sky,
And the south wind bloweth softly,
 When Thou speakest peace on high.

Quite other fields of experience are traversed in
this hermit's hymn :   .

In lonely desert place,
 Without one human friend,
If God would daily show His face,
 I could my lifetime spend:
He is in every thing,
 All-present every hour;
There is no creature that can bring
 Its strength to help His power.

The fearful desert night,
 Perils in every place,
And fear of death—all take their flight,
 Where God reveals His face:
His beauty passing fair,
 His peace, and perfect love,
Make holy festivals, where'er
 He shineth from above.

Where Thou art, in all things
Immortal life abounds;
Like streams from out the rock it springs,
And reaches heaven's bounds :
From Thee alone have come
All dawns of shining white,
To guide, through wastes and lowlands home,
The children of the light.

Ye sun and moon, farewell ;
Farewell, ye stars of night ;
Where God's sweet presence comes to dwell,
There needs no other light :
A vast eternal day
Comes from His smiling face ;
A better, greater light than they—
The radiance of His grace.

In his day the work of foreign missions was
scarcely more than a Christian dream. But it was
a dream that often filled his mind and his song.
Indeed, it is exceedingly interesting to see the
profound missionary colouring of Welsh hymns of
the last century. It was as the singing of birds in
the dawn before the sun has risen. Now that the
missionary enterprise has passed beyond a dream
—has advanced so far as to be thought fit for
arraignment—it may not be amiss to associate
our thoughts with the childlike faith and happy
dreamings of earlier days :

The glory is coming, God said it on high,
When light in the evening will break from the sky ;

The north and the south and the east and the west
With joy of salvation and peace will be blest.

The winter shall pass that has lingered so long,
Throughout the wide earth shall the birds sing Thy
    song;
The hills will be covered with harvests for Thee,
And flowers shall blossom from mountain to sea.

Thy promise shall spread over valley and hill,
Thy promise most precious of peace and good-will;
The Spirit shall gather Thy people of old,
The children of Israel, again to the fold.

The sons and the daughters shall prophesy then,
And praise and exalt the Redeemer of men;
The old men shall dream of the joys that await,
And scarcely believe when the peace is so great.

O summer of holiness! hasten along,
The purpose of glory is constant and strong:
The winter will vanish—the clouds pass away—
O South-wind of heaven, breathe softly to-day!

No one can read the Welsh hymns of the last
century without noting how every sentiment turns
lovingly to the cross. The cross absorbs the
themes of sermon and song; for it was the sun
and shield of the National Revival. There is
scarcely a hymn of Williams' in which it does not
stand forth clear and towering. The passion of
these verses is not of earth :

Who'll give me balm of Gilead—
Forgiveness, with its peace ?
Then fear of death would vanish,
My soul would be at ease :
And who can soothe the anguish
Of guilt and evil will ?
I know of none but Jesus,
Once nailed upon the hill.

Hard were the nails and cruel,
To pierce that form of grace ;
But now they hold the compass
Of heaven in its place :
The hope of Adam's children
Flows from that awful hour,
When earth beheld its Maker
Abused by human power.

If ever the authority
Of Calvary should fail,
No hope, nor any comfort,
Would then for me avail :
Most wretched, oh ! most wretched
Would I of all men be :
The dreadful grave would swallow
My soul, full surely.

Oh ! vast, and ever vaster,
The mercy He made known :
Behold, the wide creation
Doth last in Him alone :
The moan of that dark mountain—
Lama sabachthani !
Is now the pearl most precious
Of any land or sea.

Unbearable the burden
　To man—yea, to the best ;
And on my God's own shoulder
　It terribly did rest :
Justice was there demanding
　The price to be made good ;
And sin's eternal ransom
　Was paid in sweat and blood.

The vast unmeasured mountain
　Upon Himself He took,
From off the feeble shoulders
　Of guilty man forsook :
When Nature saw the burden
　Of infinite disgrace,
The very earth was shaken,
　And heaven hid its ·face.

If thousand worlds were ransomed
　By that one sacrifice,
Too dear would they be counted,
　Redeemed at such a price :
No angel can, or seraph,
　Tell e'en a thousandth part
Of that great price of ransom—
　The blood of God's own heart.

A fire in thousand bosoms
　Through heaven ravisheth—
A new white flame of wonder,
　Remembering His death :
It silences their music
　With ever new surprise :
They look on God Incarnate,
　And say—'Behold ! He dies ! '

To Thee, my God, my Saviour,
  Praise be for ever new ;
Let people come to praise Thee
  In numbers like the dew ;
Oh ! that in every meadow
  The grass were harps of gold,
To sing to Him for coming
  To ransom hosts untold !

Williams died January 11, 1791, at Panty-celyn, near Llandovery. An obituary notice, which appeared in *The Gentleman's Magazine* of that year, speaks of 'the true poetic fire, striking imagery, and glowing expressions, united with the plaintive muse of the country' in his hymns ; and says further—'His imagination gave variety and interest to his orations ; his piety was warm, yet candid and charitable ; his manners simple, yet affectionate and obliging ; and his moral conduct without blemish or imputation.' When, however, it is therein prophesied that 'he is, perhaps, the last lyric poet of South Wales, the language of the country giving way '—we learn once more that it is not wise for a prophet to prophesy aloud.

In a quiet village churchyard in the Vale of Towy, 'he awaits the coming of the Morning Star which shall usher in the glories of the first resur-rection.' So reads the inscription over his grave, written by his son. And his hymns fill the long night-watches with blessed hope, 'until the day break.'

CHAPTER IV.

ANN GRIFFITHS.

As the song of Moses was seconded by the song of Miriam, so the song of Williams, Pantycelyn, and his contemporaries was seconded by a young prophetess of Christ.

This is ANN GRIFFITHS, a farmer's daughter, born in the year 1776, at Dolwar, near Llanfyllin, in the county of Montgomery. As a young woman, she was full of gay spirits, and used to speak very flippantly of the deepened religious earnestness of the age. She used to point to the crowds of people which journeyed from all parts of the country to the Association at Bala, and say —'See the pilgrims going to Mecca.' She was extremely fond of dance and merry song and rustic gaiety.

She had gone to attend one of these merry-making festivals at Llanfyllin, when she was induced by an old servant of her father's to enter the Independent chapel. She did so without any afterthought whatever. But, like David Jones, of Cayo, she found a message waiting for her there. She did not stay for the festival, but went home

forthwith in a storm of troubled thought and dark
questionings. She went to her parish clergyman:
he met her heart-breaking distress with light jokes
and most untimely jests. Taking hold of her hand,
he said—' Let me see, Ann, if the veins of vanity
have all gone out of thy hand.' She went away
more distracted than ever. Her brother was
already one of 'the pilgrims of Mecca.' She went
with him to the chapel he frequented, and the
message of dawning hope came to her there. An
affinity of religious feelings led her soon afterwards
to join the society, and she became a strong and
shining influence in the quiet valleys around her
home.

But she was only permitted to keep the lamp
burning during the hours of a brief watch for her
Lord. She died when twenty-nine years of age,
after a married life of about ten months, and
having led a Christian life of about eight years.
And yet in another sense the lamp was never put
out at all: for hymns and letters, unsurpassed for
spiritual fervour, keep that brief life burning with
quenchless light.

The story of her first hymn beautifully images
one phase of her religion. Once, when returning
home after an exciting service, full of her own
unworthiness and of the glory of Christ, she turned
down a narrow, sheltered lane, in order to be alone
to pray. There she knelt; and in her communion
with God the spirit of sacred song touched her soul;
and by the time she reached her home she had

composed her first verse—the fourth in the following hymn :

Great Author of salvation
    And providence for man,
Thou rulest earth and heaven
    With Thy far-reaching plan :
To-day, or on the morrow,
    Whatever woe betide,
Grant us Thy strong assistance,
    Within Thy hand to hide.

What though the winds be angry,
    What though the waves be high,
While Wisdom is the ruler,
    The Lord of earth and sky !
What though the flood of evil
    Rise stormily and dark,
No soul can sink within it—
    God is Himself the ark !

Give us the faith of angels,
    That we may look and see
Salvation's depths of radiance
    And holy mystery :
Two natures in one person,
    Harmonious, part and whole :
The blood divine availing
    To ransom every soul.

My soul, behold the fitness
    Of this great Son of God ;
Trust Him for life eternal,
    And cast on Him thy load :

A Man !—touched with the pity
Of every human woe ;
A God !—to claim the kingdom,
And vanquish every foe.

One association of the first verse in the above
hymn gives it a strange pathos. A large number
of miners in a town of Glamorganshire having
been turned out of employment lately, they used
to gather in an open place for conference. The
proceedings were opened more than once by the
singing of this verse. A scene peculiarly Welsh,
surely !—and a scene aglow with the light of
heavenly romance. When their daily bread
seemed to fail them, and the world looked dark
around them, their Bible and their native song
taught them to look upward to the Author of
human Providence—in whose hand they could
verily hide without fear of evil.

But to return to the writer of the hymn and her
story : she who once laughed at the pilgrims of
Bala became now one of the most devout of them.
She used to attend there on the Communion
Sabbath, although it meant for her, as for
hundreds more, a rugged mountainous journey of
over twenty miles. Once on her way home she
became so absorbed in holy contemplation that she
rode many miles out of her way over the Berwyn
Hills before ever awakening to the fact. The
result of those hours of thought is kept in this
hymn :

Blessed day of rest eternal
From my labour, in my place !
On a shoreless sea of wonders,
The unfathomed depths of grace :
Finding an abundant entrance
To the Triune God's abode :
Seas to sail and never compass ;
God as man, and man as God.

Neither shall the sun light on them,
Nor the fear of death give pain ;
Tears forgotten in the anthem
Of the Lamb which once was slain :
Sailing on the crystal river
Of the peace of One in Three,
Underneath the cloudless beamings
Of the death of Cavalry.

Nothing could mark the intensity of feeling more strikingly than the broken sentences and rapid interchange of thoughts. ' The cloudless beamings of the death of Cavalry : '—the confused eloquence reveals the divine anguish of imagination.

Reference has been made to her letters. Their intrinsic worth, and their intimate connection with her hymns, make it unnecessary to give an excuse for a larger reference. They are the autobiography of a sacred passion, and exquisitely reflect the lights and shadows of a mind that lived within itself in Christ.

The letters were mostly written to a young friend in the ministry, and became a valuable means of unburdening a mind that was bowed down with an

exceeding weight of glory. They are the revealed
secrets of an unresting heart, told in simple and
devout speech.

The Bible was her fountain of life—a fountain
of water clear and cool as the dewdrops of a June
morning, embosomed in fadeless flowers of spring.
She drank of the living stream, she carried away
choice flowers of peace to lie close to her soul.
Her piety had in it a sweet tyranny, which compelled each verse to yield the comfort she needed
at the time. For instance, in one letter we read :

' I have had some trials like stormy winds, until
I was nearly breathless on the steep paths of the
hill; but I was brought up to the summit as
by these two chains—" A man shall be as an
hiding-place from the wind, and a covert from the
tempest ; " and—" Come, My people, enter thou
into thy chambers : hide thyself as it were for a
little moment." My spirit felt the peace and
warmth for a while.'

And in another letter :

' Lately the following words were of great value
and comfort to my soul—" Thy neck is like the
tower of David builded for an armoury, whereon
there hang a thousand buckles, all shields of
mighty men." In myself, I am but helpless and
unarmed against my foes ; but if I shall have the
privilege of turning into the tower, I shall there

find armour and strength to run through the hosts.
These words also were to me of great comfort—
"For it pleased the Father that in Him should all
fulness dwell;" and again—"A garden inclosed
is my sister, my spouse." I am greatly bound to
speak well of God, and to be grateful to Him for
some degrees of the fellowship of the mystery.
But this is my grief—I fail to stay—I am always
forsaking Him. I see how great is my loss on
that account: but more than all is the dishonour
and disrespect thrown upon God. Grant me help
to stay!'

She could even reverently thank God for using
His Word as an instrument of trouble, destroying
the strong root of self-conceit, without doing the
soul injury.

Her sacred passion brought with it a precious
pain and grief. The very fervour of her devotion
to Christ made her judge herself with all the
severity of a Paul:

'For a long time I have been sorely troubled.
I have many disappointments in myself con-
tinually; but I must say that all trials and all
storms of every kind have wrought me to this:
that is, they have brought me to see more of the
corruptions of my nature and more of the Lord in
His goodness and unchangeableness toward me.
Lately I was far from the Lord in the backsliding
of my soul; and yet I held up against His

ministry, as if I were not refusing to stay and walk in His fellowship. But for all my art, the Lord visited me in these words—"If I be a Father, where is Mine honour? and if I be a Master, where is My fear?" . . .

'In view of my path after forsaking God, and hewing out broken cisterns, this word anew raised me a little on my feet—"The Lord is my Shepherd; I shall not want." I the one going astray, He the Shepherd; I unable to return, He the Almighty Lord. Oh! Rock of our salvation! entirely dependent upon Himself, saving and cherishing sinners! I would wish to be always under the treatment, be it ever so bitter.'

This is more cheerful, but still the spiritual element is of the same self-searching earnestness:

'I feel renewed affection toward the doctrine of the Gospel, because it shows a way to cleanse the unclean. I think I have no need to change my garment, only to be purer in it. I feel a stronger longing than ever I felt before to be pure; and these words are on my mind—"And the house, when it was in building, was built of stones made ready." I feel an earnest desire to be shaped by Him, until I am made fit for the heavenly building.'

The Rev. Thomas Charles, Bala, once made a remark to her that touched her soul to the quick. Considering the depth and rareness of her experiences, and the marvellous dispensations through which God led her spirit, he said that she seemed very likely to meet with one of three things : either she would meet with severe trials, or her life would soon be ended, or she would fall back. When she heard of falling back, she burst into tears. That fear is touchingly echoed in these sentences :

'What presses most heavily on my mind at present is the sinfulness of permitting anything seen to have too large a place in my thoughts. I am reverently ashamed, and wonderingly rejoice, to think that He who humbles Himself in looking at the things of heaven has made Himself an object of love to a creature as poor as I am ; and in view of such a dishonour upon God as to give the first place to second things, I simply think that I would prefer my nature to be crushed to death (if need be), on account of its weakness to bear the heat of fiery trials. I sometimes think I could joyfully endure that, rather than the glory of God should be clouded before my mind, through granting my material nature its pomp and its desires.'

Mercifully did the Providence of God respond to her prayer.

Her mind was eager to discern the vivid outline of Christian doctrine, but mostly in its practical relations. How modestly, how devoutly she takes herself to task in these words for having unwittingly ignored the personal office of the Holy Spirit !

'The most particular thing on my mind is the great evil and great danger of grieving the Holy Ghost. The following words have struck me— " Know ye not that your body is the temple of the Holy Ghost which is in you?"

'In penetrating somewhat into the wonders of that Person, and that He dwells and abides in the believer, I simply think that I was never possessed with the same degrees of reverent fear lest He should be grieved; and along with that it was given to me to see that one cause, and the chief cause, of this great sin having such a slight impression of uneasiness on my mind was, that my thoughts about the Divine greatness of His person were too low. My whole conception of the Persons of the Trinity was too low; to think of it my mind is held with shame: but I owe it to myself to say that my mind has changed. I used to think of the Persons of the Father and Son as equal: but I held an opinion of the Person of the Holy Ghost as if He were an officer inferior to the Father and the Son. Oh! fanciful and mistaken opinion concerning One who is Divine, all-present, all-knowing, all-powerful to bring forward and perfect the good work which He has begun, according to the conditions of the covenant of grace, according to the decree of Three in One on behalf of the objects of heaven's morning Love! Oh! to be of their number! I thirst to rise higher in the belief that there is a personal indwelling of the Holy Ghost in my soul—a belief brought through revelation—not fancifully, expecting to comprehend the form and manner in which He dwells ; this would be idolatry. In considering the sinfulness in itself of grieving the Holy Ghost, and, on the other hand, in looking down to the depths of the Great Fall, and that I am dispossessed of every power, except of being able to grieve Him—my soul is sorely pressed. The following words are on my mind—" Watch and pray." As if the Lord were saying, though the commandment is strong, and thou art unable to fulfil one out of a thousand things there, on the ground where thy mind stands, go forth, prove the Throne of Grace ; for "the effectual fervent prayer of a righteous man availeth much "—" My grace is sufficient for thee: for My strength is made perfect in weakness." Blessed be the God who fulfils His promises ! '

Her hymns and her letters form an interchangeable commentary. Both are the simple and fresh outpourings of her soul. In one of her letters we find her tremulously approaching the mystery of the Creator becoming a Sufferer :

' My mind at present is looking on Jesus bearing the crown of thorns and the scarlet robe, and afterwards in His great sufferings upon the cross. It is not to be wondered at that the sun should hide its beams when its Creator was pierced with nails ! My mind stands astonished when I consider the Person who suffered on the cross—

He whose eyes are as a flame of fire piercing
through heaven and earth, at the same time
unable to see the work of His hands when darkness
was over all the earth!   My mind is overwhelmed
with too much astonishment to say any more.
No wonder that word is written down—"The Lord
is well pleased for His righteousness' sake; He
will magnify the law and make it honourable":
and the other word—"Kiss the Son, lest He be
angry." Would that the remainder of my days were
a season of unfaltering fellowship with Christ and
His sufferings, and with the Father through Him!'

The same spiritual emotion can be traced in
these verses, almost line by line:

> Heaven sweetly will remember
>   The decree of Three in One,
> Ever gazing on the Person
>   Who became a Son of Man:
> In fulfilling the conditions
>   Dying sorrow pierced His soul;
> Now the host no man can number
>   Mightily His praise extol.
>
> In remembering the battle,
>   All my tears for joy are dried;
> Free for ever stands the sinner,
>   While the law is magnified:
> For the peace of man behold Him—
>   Life's Almighty Author slain!
> And the Resurrection buried
>   For an endless human gain!

In the midst, between two robbers,
    There the great Atonement died;
And by Him the arm was strengthened
    Which could dare to pierce His side:
When His Father's law was honoured,
    And the sinner's ransom paid,
Justice stood in shining glory—
    We were free and undismayed.

King of kings, and great Rest-giver!
    See, my soul, His lowly bed!
All creation in Him movèd,
    He within the grave lay dead!
Wonder of the holy angels,
    Life of those who once were lost:
Unto Him, the God Incarnate,
    Sing the great adoring host.

Her latter days were spent close to the frontiers of the Better Land. Her soul was filled with the thoughts and desires of her eternal home. We can almost watch the flame of the spirit's life burning higher and higher—burning up the earthliness of her nature and the last remainders of unheavenly interests. Thus she writes:

'I see more need than I have ever seen before to spend what there is left of my days in giving myself daily, body and soul, to the care of Him who is able to keep that which is committed unto Him against that day. Not giving myself once, but living in giving myself, until, and even when this tabernacle is put off. The thought of putting

it off is specially sweet sometimes. I can say, it
is this of all things which gives me most joy in
these days. Not death in itself, but the great gain
to be had after passing through it; every inclination contrary to the will of God left behind, every
inclination to dishonour the ordinance of God left
behind—all infirmity swallowed up of strength—
perfectly conformable to the law—in the likeness
of God to enjoy Him for ever. I am sometimes so
carried away with these things that I fairly fail to
stand on the way of my duty in the things of time;
but waiting for the hour when I shall be dissolved
and be with Christ, for it is much better, although
it is very good with me here sometimes. When
my Beloved showeth Himself through the lattice,
He sometimes reveals, in a glass darkly, as much
of His glory to me as my feeble faculties can bear.
I rejoice to say in closing—I would wish to say it
with thankfulness—in spite of my sinfulness, and
the cunning of hell, of the world and its charms,
through the good grace of God I have not changed
the object of my affection till to-night: rather from
my heart I rest in His love, and joy over Him with
singing, although I cannot obtain that in the least
degree on this side of death, except with effort and
violence.'

And thus she sings:

Must I face the stormy river?
     There is One to break its flood—
Christ, my great High-priest and faithful,
     Christ, my all-sufficient good:

Through His blood shall come the triumph
  Over death and hell to me ;
And I shall be in His likeness,
  Sinless through eternity.

Disembodied of all evil,
  I shall pierce with earnest eyes
Into Calvary's deep wonders,
  And its infinite surprise :
The Invisible beholding,
  Who is living and was dead ;
In a pure, unbroken union
  With the ever-living Head.

There I shall exalt the Person,
  God's own Sacrifice Divine,
Without any veil or fancy—
  And my soul like Him shall shine :
With the mystery revealèd
  In His wounds, I shall commune ;
Losing sight no more for ever
  Of the all-belovèd Son.

From salvation's highest fountains,
  Oh, to drink with each new day !
Till my thirst for earthly pleasures
  Has completely passed away :
Waiting always for my Master,
  Quick to answer to His call ;
Then to hold the door wide open,
  And enjoy Him, all in all.

These letters and hymns were not written and

sung in a cloister. They are Divine breathings
rising out of the quiet stir of country life, like a
lark out of the wind-swept heather. She lived a
woman's ordinary life of a century ago. When
her mother died, she became her father's help-
mate. She was busy from morn till eve with the
daily duties of the farmstead. She had no hour
of prayer and song marked out, nor was there
any need. Her prayers accompanied the work
of her hands; her hymns were often composed in
the midst of her household tasks. She became
a 'priest unto God,' and the golden bells round
about the hem of her spirit's robe were not often
silent.

If she had a deep concern for personal piety,
she was equally concerned for social religion. A
member of the Calvinistic Methodist Church at a
place called the Bont, she carried all its joys
and sorrows in her heart. When the Church was
wounded 'by the stroke of the world and of those
falling back,' her own soul was also wounded.
Her prayers breathed revivingly on the Lord's
'faded garden.' And when the Church had its
bright awakening, her joy was full. She had
heavy and rugged paths to travel from her home
to the chapel, but the darkest winter night made
no difference to her. She could sing on the way.
It was a narrow way, too, her soul had to travel,
and she met some wintry nights of doubt before
she reached the gate of the temple. But she sang
for the Light that was to come.

There's a day to journey homewards
  For the children of the King ;
God shall from the fields of bondage
  To the throne His loved ones bring :
There shall faith to sight be changèd,
  Feeble hope to perfect gain ;
And the song shall grow for ever
  To the Lamb which once was slain.

Pilgrim, worn with stress of tempests,
  Look, and see the dawning light !
There the Lamb makes intercession,
  In His flowing robes of white :
Faithfulness, His golden girdle ;
  Round His garment's hem, the bells ;
Token of the full forgiveness
  Which in His atonement dwells.

A noteworthy fact in connection with her hymns
is their preservation. A servant in her father's
house, named Ruth, possessed a remarkable
memory. To her Ann Griffiths used to recite her
hymns as they were composed ; and then the two
would sing them over time after time. After the
death of the young authoress, Ruth used to repeat
these verses to her husband. He saw their worth,
and wrote them down from her dictation. To-day
they cannot be lost : they have a home in too
many hearts.

CHAPTER V.

WE are still in the eighteenth century; and we must linger in the romantic though little known Vale of Towy, to make the acquaintance of two more sacred poets of Wales. One of these is MORGAN RHYS, the story of whose life is almost entirely lost. We have, however, the memoir of his soul safely kept in his hymns and elegies. Being a contemporary and neighbour of David Jones and William Williams, he seems to have felt the stress and storm of the same religious conflict; and his devotion has very much of the same deep and fervent colour. He was influenced largely by the potent spirit of Griffith Jones, of Llanddowror, the Morning Star of the Great Revival; and for a time undertook the care of one of his Circulating Schools.

These schools were instituted to impart the simplest forms of elementary knowledge in country villages. After a schoolmaster had been for a while engaged in removing the dense ignorance of one district, he had to leave it for another; so the 'little knowledge' was scattered far and wide, although in very small instalments. In the latter part of his life, Mr. Rhys established a stationary school on his own responsibility : most probably in order that he might have more of personal freedom in his evangelistic work. For he was one of the band of Calvinistic Methodist itinerant preachers that rendered noble service in that age to the renaissance of national piety. His hymns reflect strongly the theological lights and shades of his day ; when the human side of Redemption was to a very considerable extent ignored, so as to emphasize the divine side of it. The total depravity of man—the impossibility of salvation by means of legal obedience—the need of the atonement, and its sufficiency—these are the doctrines which his harp translates into song. When he once went to Williams, Pantycelyn, and read out to him one of his hymns, that master of sacred song told him that it contained the experience of a ' good Christian and a half.' His hymns reveal a mind dwelling much in pleasant melancholy, as in the shadow of leafy branches flecked with sunlight.

I promise every day
To keep the narrow way,
    But daily fail :
God of the bush of yore,
Strengthen me more and more ;
If Thou but walk before,
    I shall prevail.

A thousand evil foes
Around my pathway close,
    And I am weak :
Give me Thy hand, I pray,
To hold me in the way ;
And in the latter day,
    Lord, for me speak !

In the two following verses we seem to hear the far-off noise of battle—a dim echo from the theological conflicts of bygone days, when the term 'Antinomian' was a favourite missile to hurl at an opponent.

All praise to Christ the Righteous
    Who for my sin has died,
And from the grave has risen
    That I be justified :
Upon His throne of pity
    He intercedes for me,
And names His life of sorrow,
    His death upon the tree.

Now in the face of Moses,
    No friend shall have my plea :
But Jesus Christ the Righteous
    Who died for one like me !
In Jordan's swelling torrent,
    Or in that 'day to come,'
I know His hand will hold me,
    And safely bring me home.

'Now in the face of Moses,' has in it the martial ring of some famous old battle-cry.

A similar theme is handled in these glowing verses:

Lord, open mine eyes to behold
　　The worth of Thy wondrous decree:
Far better than silver and gold,
　　The law of Thy mouth is to me:
The fire shall consume all below,
　　But Thou art the same, and Thy plan—
'Tis life everlasting to know
　　My Saviour as God and as Man.

O wonder of infinite cost!
　　The way that He took in His grace,
To rescue a man that was lost,
　　By dying Himself in His place!
He conquered the serpent's despite,
　　And stood there alone as my King!
He leadeth us now in His might—
　　Let those on the Rock shout and sing.

The Mighty One has overcome,
　　His foes in confusion retire;
And Zion is on its way home
　　In terrible chariots of fire;
The saints and the angels unite,
　　A white-shining numberless throng,
To bear through the realms of the light,
　　To Him the all-conquering song.

The other illustration from the hymns of Morgan Rhys comes in less familiar form:

O welcome, blessed morrow !
No foe, nor any sorrow
   Can reach the land of life :
     The conquering throng
     Shall gather with song,
   From all this world of strife

In Salem's tranquil regions
No sound of warring legions
   Breaks on the music fair :
     The Saviour will be
     My heaven for me—
   And no one sinneth there !

The grave will be so peaceful,
Until the dawning blissful
   Shall wake me from my rest :
     And then I shall rise
     With joy to the skies,
   In Jesu's likeness drest.

There is the crown of brightness,
And robes of purest whiteness,
   And holy festival :
     No evil is there,
     No enemy dare
   Approach its pearlèd wall.

There God is ever glorious,
The Lamb is all-victorious,
   O blessed Three in One !
     My soul was a brand
     Plucked out by His hand—
   When shall His praise be done ?

Another schoolmaster under Griffith Jones, and a maker of sacred songs also, was DAVID WILLIAMS, who was born near Llandovery, in the year 1718; and died October 1, 1794, at Llandilo-fach, in the county of Glamorgan. Very little is known of him; and it seems probable that still less would be known, were it not for the severity of his domestic trials. His wife was an advanced pupil of the school of Xantippe; and her violent temper kept the poet's sensitive spirit in exquisite torment. Among other troubles, he had to change his denomination on her account. But whatever of that, as in the case of another sweet singer who had to practise 'on an evil spirit,' his harp lost none of its tenderness of devotion. Some of his verses rank among the best in Welsh hymnology; and one especially is known wherever the Welsh tongue is spoken. He has not enclosed so much systematic theology in his hymns as Morgan Rhys: rather is he the minstrel of the mortal strife of men, with their sorrow and joy and divine endeavour. Many a troubled soul can join him in this remonstrance with doubt:

> Unbelief, let me have quiet,
>   Else my cry of pain shall rise
> From this valley of affliction
>   To the gracious dawning skies:
> There for me my Brother pleadeth,
>   Unforgetting day or night:
> He will come and break my fetters,
>   He will lead me into light.

Little Faith, where art thou hiding ?
　For thy ministry take heart :
Why, sweet Hope, art thou so timid ?
　For the feeble do thy part :
Soon the battle will be over—
　Unbelief, away ! away !
Though I am so faint and helpless,
　I am gaining ground each day.

In another hymn we are still touched with the
anguish of the strife :

Hear my grief ! believe I cannot
　That for me there is a hope,
Who, between two weak opinions
　Halting, in the darkness grope :
Fearing much and trusting little,
　Shall I stand at last or fall ?
Fearing evil hosts of darkness,
　Fearing self the most of all !

Sometimes in the gloomy valley,
　Sometimes on the sunny height ;
Sometimes drinking Marah's waters,
　Sometimes wine of pure delight :
Sometimes sighs and bitter moanings,
　Sometimes joy on every string ;
Sometimes low beneath the billows,
　Sometimes sunward on my wing.

I am trusting, come what happen,
　Trusting in the word of grace—
That the riven Rock of Ages
　Is my perfect hiding-place :

In the cleft there is a Refuge,
  In the cleft is sweetest calm ;
In the cleft alone is safety—
  Wounds of Christ, unblemished Lamb.

In most of his hymns he keeps the same figure
or phrase through all his verses.   In the following
he sings of the ' breezes of Mount Zion ' :

Lord, let the gladdening breezes
  Revive this soul of mine,
And raise it, weak and wearied,
  To heaven's air benign :
The breeze will break and scatter
  The clouds that hang so low;
I long to feel its freshness—
  From heaven let it blow !

The breezes of Mount Zion
  Kindle the holy flame ;
The breezes of Mount Zion
  Renew the feeble frame :
Oft in the breeze of Zion
  My soul with song would fill ;
And I shall yet be singing,
  Before I reach the hill.

The breezes of Mount Zion
  Shall fill the sails again ;
And lift the stranded vessel
  To voyage o'er the main :
The breezes of Mount Zion
  Leave all the sky aglow ;—
In Canaan's sunny valleys
  No cold winds ever blow.

It must have been during one of his sunward
flights that he saw this radiant vision of Eternal
Love standing in the midst of all change without
a cloud on its brow, without a fear in its soul :

> Oh ! the grace no will can conquer !
>   The omnipotence of love !
> Changeless is my Father's promise,
>   It will never, never move :
> In the storm this is my anchor—
>   God can never change His mind ;
> In the wounds of Christ He promised
>   Life to me : and He is kind.

But the verse that has undoubtedly travelled
wherever the Welsh language has, is the one of
which I give the first line as it stands in the
original :

Yn y dyfroedd mawr a'r tonnau.

It is the popular tradition that one stormy night,
on reaching home after having been away preaching, he was hailed with all the bitterness the
practised tongue of his wife could command.   It
was more than he could bear : he preferred the
company of the storm without to the mad rhetoric
within, so away he went, and stood on the banks
of the River Llwchwr. The rush of the raging
torrent and the noise of the wild night brought
to his mind another river and another night, when
his soul would be overwhelmed by the desolate
presence of death.   What hope would remain loyal
then ? What help would be at hand ?

In the waves and mighty waters
   No one will support my head,
But my Saviour, my Belovèd,
   Who was stricken in my stead :
In the cold and mortal river
   He will hold my head above ;
I shall through the waves go singing
   For one look of Him I love !

A touching incident has given to this verse the title of 'The Miners' Hymn.' In the month of April, 1877, a colliery at Cymmer, in the Rhondda Valley, was flooded, and fourteen miners found themselves in a prison of darkness and terror, waiting helplessly for death. The whole nation seemed to turn its thought towards that coal-pit, and every day made the suspense more painful. The rescue-party toiled manfully day and night; and when seven days had passed without any reward to their labour, the last hope was almost given up. But on the eighth day nine of those imprisoned were found : and they were alive, though exhausted to the verge of death. Without air, without food, despair would have driven them mad were it not for the above hymn, which they sang over and over again with a feeling of terrible reality. 'The waves and mighty waters' were there ; so was their Saviour, their Beloved. And they sang for one look of Him !

The Rev. BENJAMIN FRANCIS was born at Pengelli, near Newcastle-Emlyn, in the year 1734. His father was a Baptist minister, a man of large

talents and many labours, his name being associated with the origin of several churches on the
confines of the three counties of Cardigan, Caermarthen, and Pembroke. The son spoken of here
was only six years old when his father died ; but
there were faithful friends who cared for him till
he could care for himself. He commenced preaching at the age of nineteen ; and soon after he
entered the Academy at Bristol. In the year 1758
he was ordained minister of the Baptist church at
Horsley, in Gloucestershire ; and there he laboured
in Christ for nearly half a century—until he was
called to rest. His love for his native land con-
strained him to make contributions towards its
church-song. His hymns are very correct and
well finished ; but only a few of them have found a
permanent place in the sanctuary. Even these do
not lend themselves to translation, being mostly free
versions of the Psalms or of English hymns. He
also published several English hymns ; of which
two at least are fairly well known—although in each
case there is some confusion as to the authorship.

Hark ! the voice of love and mercy

is generally attributed to him, with a query on
behalf of the Rev. Jonathan Evans.

Jesus ! and shall it ever be

is again put down to Grigg, but altered by
Benjamin Francis.

CHAPTER VI.

*THOMAS WILLIAMS—CHARLES O'R BALA—
DAVID CHARLES.*

With the close of the eighteenth century the
Golden Age of Welsh hymnody began to decline.
There has been a succession of great national poets
since ; but they are bards of the Eisteddvod rather
than singers of the sanctuary. . At the same time
it deserves to be noted that the chief Eisteddvod
poems of the present century have nearly all
some sacred subject. The great poets have failed,
as usual, to write great hymns. Still, the period is
not void of interesting illustrations of the songs of
the Church.

Thomas Williams, of Bethesda, in the Vale of
Glamorgan, was originally a well-to-do farmer ;
but, owing to a bitter controversy concerning the
alleged heresy of an eminent Methodist divine of
the time—the Rev. Peter Williams—he, with a
number of sympathizers, organized an Independent church, of which he afterwards became
minister. Religiously, he was a child of the
eighteenth century ; and his hymns have a close
spiritual affinity to the hymns of David Jones and

Morgan Rhys and William Williams. But here and
there we find traces of the natural reaction which
followed the fervour of the Great Revival. A chill
melancholy steals sometimes over his faith—like
the sound of an autumn breeze shuddering among
the brown leaves after sunset. But it passes, and
he rejoices again. His volume of hymns, entitled
Waters of Bethesda, was published in 1823. It
takes its name from its first, and one of his best-
known hymns.

> I also, like so many more,
>   Am here beside the pool ;
> Waiting the Holy Ghost to stir
>   These waters deep and cool.
>
> Within salvation's crystal flood,
>   Through time's long ages proved,
> How many hearts found health again,
>   And all disease removed !
>
> Beside the pool for many a day
>   My soul has been in grief ;
> And every hour is like a year,
>   In waiting God's relief.
>
> And shall it be that I must die,
>   Who have remained so long ?
> Before me others always go
>   And wash, and they are strong.
>
> I was the first of all to come,
>   But they were first made whole !
> When shall the day of healing dawn
>   On *my* unhappy soul ?

Here I shall tarry, come what may,
    For who is there can tell
But the Physician will Himself
    Come soon, and make me well?

Some of his best-known hymns—as in the case
of nearly all Welsh hymn-writers—relate the vision
of death : the favourite theme being that of
natural fear gradually overcome by the Christian
faith, as in the following :

Where is Elijah's God?
    Wilt Thou not come at length?
For all my hope and stay
    Is only in Thy strength :
The fathers I have loved are gone;
I have but Thee to lead me on.

The breeze is blowing chill
    Since early afternoon;
And as I feel its cold
    I know that Death comes soon :
Nought but Thy peace can take away
The grave's dark sorrow and dismay.

The river is at hand,
    I see its highest wave :
And how can one so weak
    Its stormy torrents brave ?
God of Elijah, come once more,
Divide the waters as of yore !

Confirm my feeble faith,
  So fearful to advance—
Afraid to trust the word
  That never failed me once!
And Christ is in His sovereign right,
The resurrection's Life and Light.

O morning full of peace!
  Its light is in the skies;
The prisons of the grave
  Shall fall, and never rise:
Nor death nor grave shall then be known,
From dawn till eve, from eve till dawn.

It would not be well to pass from him without
including this little hymn; so simple in form, and
its thought so sunny:

The Tree of Life in barren soil
  At length has taken root,
And bends its branches to the ground,
  That all may taste its fruit.

Through wintry months of dark and cold,
  The fruit is on it still;
Its leaves bring healing to the wounds
  Of mind and heart and will.

If on this side the stream we find
  The fruit of Christ so good,
It will be better, better far,
  The other side the flood.

When strength has failed within my heart,
  When human help is past,
In Thine own bosom, Jesu, Lord,
  Grant me to rest at last.

In the good Providence of God the national
revival of the eighteenth century was followed by
a period of wise constructive energy. After the
solemn awakening came the broad and sober reign
of education. Catechisms were used largely, and
with much profit: theology was organized, and
church polity was defined. Among those approved
workmen in constructive religion, no name is more
honoured than that of CHARLES O'R BALA. The
memorable little incident of 'Mary Jones and her
Bible' has made him known everywhere as the
pioneer and one of the founders of the British and
Foreign Bible Society. He was born at Pant-dwvn,
in the county of Caermarthen, October 14, 1755, of
a respectable family of farmers. He came under
the influence of the new religious movement in the
days of boyhood, and it left a deep and permanent
impression upon his spirit. Having taken his
degree at Oxford, he was ordained priest May 21,
1780, and spent the next three years in a curacy at
Halifax. Afterwards he returned to Wales, having
been appointed to the curacy of Llanymowddwy: but
his work there came suddenly to a close. Some of
the parishioners, in their zeal for national ignorance,
accused him of giving free instruction to the children after vespers. His rector considered this to

be such a shocking innovation that he was at once
dismissed.   Like many another earnest spirit of
the time, he had to forsake the Church of his
fathers in order to have a free field for his heroic
devotion.   He publicly joined the Calvinistic Methodist movement, and found the work was 'great and
large.'   John Newton had asked him to come over
to England : but he preferred to stay at home and
bear the cross in his native land.   His splendid
toil in the interest of elementary and religious
education, his part in the founding of the Bible
Society, his Catechism and Bible Dictionary—both
of them still treasures of the household and the
Church—need only be mentioned here.[1]   One bitterly
cold night in the winter of 1799–80, he was returning over the mountains from Carnarvonshire to
Bala, when his hand was bitten by the frost, and
a severe illness succeeded.   Much prayer was made
on his behalf: but in the annals of those prayers
nothing is more remarkable than this strange
petition of one old Christian—'Fifteen years more,
O Lord !   We pray for fifteen years to be added to
the days of his life ; and wilt Thou not grant fifteen
years, O our God, for the sake of Thy Church and
Thy cause ? '   Nearly fifteen years later—in the
summer of 1814—he told his wife at Barmouth,
'Well, Sali, the fifteen years are nearly up.'   A
few weeks later, a friend called to see him one
morning, and said, 'Well, Mr. Charles, the day of

---

[1] See 'Short Biographies for the People': *Thomas
Charles*, by Rev. Dr. Herber Evans.

trouble is come!' And he answered, 'There is
Refuge!' His first word after that was spoken
beyond the veil. What better mapping out of
his spiritual course than these verses from his
only hymn, written early in the fifteen years'
trial?

O Salvation, full Salvation,
   Love's device for man's release!
What can shake the firm foundation
   Of this covenant of peace?
Here my soul in trouble resteth,
   Here through life is my abode:
When the stormy wind molesteth,
   Days of calm have I with God.

Should my health be from me taken,
   And my very life be done;
The decree remains unshaken
   Made of old by Three in One:
Unremoved the promise liveth,
   And the counsel standeth fast;
Unto him who now believeth
   Christ is life, and death is past.

Bitter things are changed to sweetness,
   Darkness into clearest day;
Trials give my spirit meetness,
   And they soon shall pass away:
By the covenant sustainèd,
   Strong in comfort shall I be,
Till my soul at last hath gainèd
   What my Father willed for me.

Once, I thought my little vessel
　Had the wild waves overpast ;
I was in the tranquil haven,
　And my anchor had been cast !
Then I cried in fear, ' My Father,
　Wilt Thou drive me back again ?
In Thy bosom take me rather,
　Let me bid farewell to pain !'

'Hush, My child, and wait My leisure,
　Know there is no God but Me ;
Be at rest in My good pleasure,
　Trust My care—My care for thee :
In the struggle I shall hide thee
　From the evil hand of foes ;
I shall always walk beside thee,
　I, thy succour and repose.'

Lord, it is enough for ever,
　If Thou only be my God ;
For Thy Son didst Thou deliver
　To redeem me with His blood :
In His shelter I have hidden,
　In the mortal bruise divine ;
Be all other joys forbidden,
　But the joy that He is mine.

The youngest brother of the above—Rev. DAVID
CHARLES, of Caermarthen—has the Christ-given
honour of having written one of the foremost
hymns in the language. He was born in 1762 ;
and, like his brother, he was under spiritual im-

pression from early childhood. During the days
of his apprenticeship he learnt by heart the whole
of Young's *Night Thoughts*. A book, and an
English book, was also the means of helping him
to final decision for Christ—the sermons of Ralph
Erskine. He spent several years of his young
manhood in Bristol; and all these English influences served him well in after years, enabling
him to preach effectively in both languages. He
preached several times with and for Rowland Hill
in Gloucestershire; and twice at least he occupied
the famous pulpit of Surrey Chapel. He was a
true builder of the churches; and early Methodism
in Wales owed a great deal to his soberness and
wisdom.

He wrote several hymns, but one has singled
itself out from among the rest. The biography of
'*O fryniau Caersalem ceir gweled*,' like that of the
'Miners' Hymn' already referred to, can only be
written in the light of the Home-land. The poet
had heard 'the shout of them that triumph,' and
he was no longer afraid of the weariness and per-
plexity of his pilgrimage in the desert. Some day
he would reach the cloudless hills of Zion, and look
back on the meanderings of the journey, to find that
it was the nearest way home.

> To us from the desert ascending
>   God giveth in Paradise rest;
> Our soul after weary contending
>   Shall peacefully lean on His breast:

7

There we shall escape from affliction,
  From sin with its shame and its pain;
Enjoying the full benediction,
  The love of the Lamb that was slain.

From the hills of the Beautiful City
  The way of the desert is clear;
What joy will be there in reviewing
  The journey's meanderings here!
To look on the storms as they gather,
  On terrible death and the grave;
While we shall be safe with the Father,
  In peace on love's shadowless wave.

While dying lips have murmured in anticipation
this joy of the heavenly retrospect from the hills of
the City, the gate of pearl has opened to many a
soul; and the faltering strain of earth has glided
imperceptibly into the choral song of seraphim and
saints redeemed.

CHAPTER VII.

THE sacred singers grouped together in this chapter had one quality in common: they were extravagantly fond of intricate rhymes and peculiar metres. This has seriously limited the use of their hymns, except in rare instances. Like Captain Middleton's Psalter, the greatest portion of their verse is so much fruitless piety; leaving, however, a saving remainder of serviceable work.

HUGH JONES (of Maesglasau), son of a well-to-do farmer, was born in the neighbourhood of Dinas Mawddwy, Merioneth, in the year 1749. He spent the life of a literary recluse, devoting himself and losing his money in enriching the literature of Wales. Among the books he translated into Welsh were the works of Josephus. He also interested himself in church psalmody, and wrote several psalm-tunes. His name lives, however, more in one hymn he wrote than in all his other work. The following is an attempted rendering of it:

Remove
The veil in this dear Mount of love,
And let the sun stand still above
  Where once, reprovèd and beshrewed,
The Lamb of God was made to feel
  The piercing steel, for my great good.

For me
No refuge anywhere can be,
But in His wounds on Calvary:
  A fount I see in that dear side
Which hath received the cruel spear—
  My soul, draw near the healing tide.

Mine, mine,
The virtue of that cross of Thine,
To cleanse my soul from evil sign:
  The woe divine—the tearful plea
Incessant at the throne of light—
  Have won the right of heaven for me.

Oh, cleanse
My life of every sinful sense
In that pure stream of innocence—
  My sole defence and benison:
Its tide shall never ebb again,
  But shall remain when time is done.

EDWARD JONES (*Maesyplwm*) was born near
the town of Denbigh, March 19, 1761. He had
the misfortune to lose his father when about ten
years old, and the far worse misfortune—to come
in early youth under the influences of evil com-
panionship. He was twenty-six years old before

he joined a Christian church, being one out of about fifteen members of the Calvinistic Methodist communion who were accustomed to hold their services in the parlour of a farmhouse. From that time he became a very useful worker. In spite of having received but few advantages of early education, he had used his native talent so wisely as to be able to add to the occupation of a farmer that of a village schoolmaster. He was more or less a verse-maker from his childhood, amusing his father with making verses when, a boy of six, he led the oxen at the plough. He died at Cilcain, near Mold, December 27, 1836. One of his carols was a great favourite of the famous Welsh preacher, Christmas Evans, who used at times to repeat portions of it in his sermons with most powerful effect. The hymn rendered below is one of his best :

All heaven and earth are filled with God,
　　Hell knows His present sight;
Eternity is His abode,
　　His name the Infinite :
He fills all distances of space,
And reigns almighty as He lists;
His years, His strength can grow no less,
　　He in Himself exists.

Existing in Himself, before
　　He framed the depth, the height,
Beyond the past eternal shore,
　　He was the Infinite ;

Without beginning of His days,
No end of life to Him can be;
Eternal still in all His ways,
    The Perfect Trinity.

There is no measure of His grace,
    And therefore it is well;
We have been told His wondrous praise,
    His rule invisible:
And as we heard, so have we seen
The endless marvels of His plan:
Unchangeable His truth has been,
    Though great the sin of man.

No spirit bright is left to faint,
    Of His regard denied;
No angel, no redeemèd saint
    But in His care abide:
Each in His presence stands revealed,
To His good pleasure consecrate;
Their comely praise to Him they yield,
    And magnify their state.

We too on earth are seen to stand
    For ever in His sight;
We live in Him, we feel His hand
    In darkness as in light:
He knows what secret sin we bear,
He watches all we do amiss;
For at each moment everywhere
    In heaven and earth He is.

Each evil thought or good unknown
    Lies open to His eye;
He hears the sigh, the silent moan,
    As well as terror's cry:

He takes the heart of man to read,
He knows how empty each design:
The wish undone is as a deed,
    Writ in the book divine.

My soul, thou art a Father's care,
    He sees thy purpose weak:
Thou hast a Brother pleading there
    Before thou ever speak:
Thy Father—He will not despise
To hear desire's softest call;
Although thy lips be dumb, His eyes
    Can see and pity all.

When in some secret place I mourn
    Beneath some cross of care,
By heavy burdens overborne,
    Too hard for me to bear;
One memory will cheer me still—
To God's dear Son my state is known;
I shall not always bear this ill,
    A better life will dawn.

PETER JONES (*Pedr Fardd*) was born in the parish of Dolbenmaen, Caernarvonshire, May 7, 1775; but in his early youth he removed to Liverpool, and spent the remainder of his days there till his death on the 26th of January, 1845. He was connected with the Welsh Calvinistic Church at Pall Mall, and exercised a large power for good among his countrymen in the city. He was especially a friend and teacher of young men, both in literature and religion. One of his best known hymns is a hymn of youth:

Now let the firstfruits of our days
Be sacred to the Saviour's praise;
The pleasure of His work is more
Than earth can bring from all its store.

Early beneath His yoke to be
Is better far than vanity;
The paths of wisdom yield each day
The peace that passeth not away.

Oh ! that my youth were wholly spent
Beneath His yoke in calm content :
For He who bought me on the tree
Owns every hour of life from me.

From among his more mechanical hymns the
following is chosen :

Sweet streams of pleasantness
    Came flowing free,
Our stricken life to bless,
    From heaven's decree :
Salvation's early thought
    Passed o'er the desert place,
And thousand blessings brought—
    Oh ! wondrous grace !

Christ made His very own
    Our mortal frame,
And for His saints He won
    A glorious claim :
Of His good-will came He
    To take a servant's place ;
Fruit of the great decree—
    Oh ! wondrous grace !

Our Helper in our stead
  Was sacrificed;
He bruised the serpent's head—
  Our Rock is Christ:
Ended is sin's control;
  We yet shall see His face,
His likeness in our soul—
  Oh! wondrous grace!

Grapes from the thorns were found
  Upon the cross;
Balm from the cruel wound,
  To heal His foes:
Soon shall our song arise,
  In endless joy of praise,
To Christ, our Sacrifice—
  Oh! wondrous grace!

ROBERT WILLIAMS (*R. ab Gwilym Ddu*) was
born in the parish of Llanystumdwy, Caernarvonshire, in the year 1767. He spent his life on his
own farm, removed far from the world, in the
company of Arvon's mountains. His days seem
to have passed by evenly till the death of his
only daughter, the child of his old age, in her
seventeenth year. His heart never recovered from
the sorrow; and the elegy he wrote on her death
is an expression of most vivid grief. He and
another famous bard—Dewi Wyn o Eifion—were
Baptists; and by their efforts a chapel was built,
which still goes by the name of 'The Bards'
Chapel.' He died June 11, 1850. The original
of the following hymn has woven itself around

some of the tenderest recollections of Welsh communion services :

From age to age the memory
  Of Jesu's blood grows fonder;
Too short eternity will be
  To tell of all its wonder.

The chiefest theme of heavenly song
  Is Jesu's dying glory;
In highest hymn each harp is strong
  To tell again the story.

The virtue of His sufferings,
  His grief in our restoring,
Sound louder on celestial strings
  Than seraphim adoring.

The song will but begin to rise
  When ages vast are over;
For ever shall His sacrifice
  New miracles discover.

When these shall reach the sacred hill,
  The sons of tribulation;
Then every string Divine shall thrill
  With louder exultation.

The music shall for ever swell,
  Host unto host replying;
But oh! the song will never tell
  The worth of Jesus dying.

CHAPTER VIII.

DANIEL DDU—NICANDER—IEUAN GLAN GEIRIONYDD.

THE REV. DANIEL EVANS (*Daniel Ddu*) was born at Llanfihangel-Ystrad, in the county of Cardigan, in the year 1792. He studied at Oxford, and afterwards became a Fellow of Jesus College. He used to spend much of his time between the terms in the neighbourhood of his birth, where he was half worshipped by the peasantry. They held some strange notions with regard to Oxford; and nothing could put out of their heads the belief that its ancient colleges were the favourite haunts of a motley crew of ghosts of a very doubtful character. He himself was considered an expert in 'raising spirits'; and as to his familiarity with the 'black art'—how could there be a doubt of it, when he could speak Latin as well as Mephistopheles himself? If he never abused his power to do them ill, it was only another proof of his good nature. In the latter part of his life he was much troubled with melancholy, and died when he was fifty-four years of age. He wrote some very successful

Eisteddvodic poetry; but nothing that he has written is so well known as the following hymn-poem on the Prodigal Son, with its effective arrangement of light and shade. Its dramatic cast stands in the way of its being used as a whole; but some of the verses are extensively known.

Who is yonder weary pilgrim
  From the desert now appears,
Coming home with cheerless footsteps,
  And his cheek bedewed with tears?
Worn and tattered is his garment,
  There is famine in his face:
Peace has made a vain endeavour
  In his heart to find a place.

Hear him to himself bemoaning—
  'Father! in Thy house make me
But a servant!—me, unworthy
  Any more Thy son to be!'
What is this—this strain celestial
  Now I hear above the sky?
Harps ten thousand times ten thousand
  In sweet harmony on high?

Oh! the softly flowing echo
  From the instruments of gold:
'Journey on, thou weary pilgrim,
  Welcome home from deserts cold!
The inhabitants of Light-land
  Now with joy thy spirit greet:
See, the robe is ready for thee—
  Soon shalt thou the Father meet.

' Journey on, thou weary pilgrim,
  Through the desert journey on ;
Though thy face is marked with sorrow,
  Song for weeping cometh soon :
Heaven's eyes watch every footstep,
  Haste thee on, O sorely tried !
Flow, ye tears, a little longer,
  Till at home ye shall be dried.'

Who is He that brings the garment
  Beautiful as light of dawn ?
Kisses him, the weary lost one,
  To His bosom closely drawn ?
Loud and louder swells the music
  Of each glowing golden string :
Little soul, art thou so precious
  In the palace of the King ?

Yes, there will be joy in heaven,
  If from evil ways thou flee
There is always, always welcome
  In the Father's house for thee :
Leave the husks and vanished shadows,
  And a world of falsehood spurn :
Thine the fulness and affection,
  Thine the home : return ! return !

Two other clergymen of the Established Church
in Wales have rendered valued service to the
national psalmody. One of these is the Rev.
MORRIS WILLIAMS (*Nicander*), who, in the spirit of
the High Church revival, published *The Church's
Year*. He also undertook a new version of the

Psalms ; but he did not succeed in supplanting the old Psalter of Edmund Prys. Like almost all the hymn-writers of this century, his best work in poetry belongs to the Eisteddvod. From his seventeenth year, when he came into notice through a poetical curiosity—a metrical ode made up entirely of Biblical proper names—from thence up to the close of his life, he made large contributions to native literature. He had come personally under the influence of the Oxford movement ; and he worked manfully for the revival of his Church in his native land. His labour, and that of like-minded men, was not in vain : the results of his devotion have reached wide and far.

The Church's Year (*Y Flwyddyn Eglwysig*) was published in 1843, reflecting in every part the influence of Keble's *Christian Year*. How far he copied the original, and where he added something of his own, may be judged from a comparison of the following hymn for Quinquagesima Sunday with that of Keble—both being based on the rainbow in Noah's covenant (Gen. ix. 13).

> Noah beheld the wondrous sign
>   On darksome clouds reclining ;
> God's peace and covenant benign
>   Were through its glory shining.
>
> As mounts the lark to yonder sky
>   Whene'er the rain is ended,
> So from the earth again made dry
>   Their song to God ascended.

The Lord Himself in heaven wrote
   His peace in one bright letter :
Expression of a tranquil thought—
   Give grace to read it better !

Bow of the covenant of grace,
   God's loving-kindness sent it !
The earth it seemeth to embrace—
   The hands of God have bent it !

My Father's flaming bow I sing,
   Its flame in love was given :
Inwrought with peace and void of string,
   No arrow from it driven !

As Jacob's ladder showed erewhile
   Heaven and earth in union ;
The frowning cloud, the sunny smile,
   Are here in calm communion.

Type of the Saviour, God and Man,
   The Rainbow o'er us bending ;
He made the earth and heaven one
   In peace that hath no ending.

How can I bear the sun's strong light ?
   The rainbowed cloud is dearer :
O Son of God ! too far, too bright—
   The Son of Man comes nearer.

This other and simpler hymn is for St. Philip
and St. James's Day—'I am the way, the truth,
and the life.'

Christ opened on the tree
　A way to heaven's door ;
And Thou Thyself, O Jesus, art
　The Way for evermore.

Truth is the homeward way
　These erring feet must wend ;
And Thou art still the Perfect Truth,
　O Jesu, dearest Friend.

The way is life indeed
　To all that walk therein ;
And Thou, O Christ, art very Life,
　Who savest us from sin.

Give grace to keep the Way,
　The paths of Truth made straight :
And follow as Thy flock before,
　Until we reach the gate.

Give strength to keep the Way,
　Heedless of human sign :
Where Thou hast walked let me be led,
　Thy very steps be mine !

While the services of Nicander, from their very
purpose and form, were largely confined to the
psalmody of his own Church, another clergyman
—the Rev. EVAN EVANS (*Ieuan Glan Geirionydd*)—
has given some choice hymns to the nation at
large. He was born at Trefriw, and had his early
imagination charmed by the picturesque surround-
ings of his home. His parents were renowned for
their piety, and were the pioneers of Calvinistic.

Methodism in the neighbourhood. Like most great men, he owed his greatness largely to his mother. He started life as a schoolmaster; but a marked success at an Eisteddvod having brought him into public notice, he was induced to devote himself to the ministry of the Church. He held successively the curacies of Christleton and Ince, in Cheshire. Ill-health compelled him to leave Ince, and he spent some time in retirement among the beloved hills of Trefriw. When he had partially recovered, he was appointed to the curacy of Rhyl. This took place in the month of July, 1854. On the 21st day of the following January death came and led him into rest.

Nearly all his hymns are prayers—prayers full of the tenderest appeals, as if his faith trembled in approaching the Golden Gate. The following is given as an instance :

> To Him who bends to hear the weak,
>   I bring my simple plea :
> In every pain and sore distress,
>   Turn not away from me !
>
> Although unworthy to enjoy
>   Thy presence full and free,
> Deserving but to be cast out—
>   Turn not away from me !
>
> When my acquaintance, one by one,
>   Leave me in misery ;
> And friend and comrade stand afar,
>   Turn not away from me !

For Thy dear cross and precious death
  On lonely Calvary,
And for Thine intercession now,
  Turn not away from me!

When I must face the stormy flood,
  Where many sorrows be;
And through the valley walk alone,
  Turn not away from me!

When Thou shalt come the second time,
  With awful majesty,
To judge the living and the dead,
  Turn not away from me!

The technical intricacies of these two verses
have not debarred them from the attainment of
wide popularity:

My race beneath the sun
  Is very nearly run;
Life fades away in sad decay,
  Soon shall my day be done:
My fragile tent is sorely rent,
  My strength is spent well-nigh;
The hour is near—I must appear
In doubt and fear within the clear
  Immortal sphere on high.

Grant, Lord, Thy peace to me,
  And Thy dear face to see;
Before my day has passed away,
  All sinless may I be!

Thy gracious light in death's dark night
 Shall soon my fright dispel :
In Thy right hand on yonder strand,
Where fears disband my soul shall stand—
 Sweet land! where all is well!

While for years the thought of death was so
present to his mind, it was natural for him to
sing this wistful :

I linger sadly near
 The stormy river ;
And long to cross, but fear
 Lest none deliver :
Oh! that I might but soar
Above its rush and roar,
And on the other shore
 Be safe for ever!

From every dismal wave
 Come dark foretellings ;
I think of all the brave
 Lost in its swellings :
O soul of mine, so frail!
What if the flood prevail,
And thou at last should'st fail
 To reach those dwellings !

But see! from yonder shore
 On high ascended,
My comrades in the war,
 Their sorrow ended :

Why should I feel alarm ?
They crossed on Jesu's arm,
And I shall know no harm,
    By Him befriended.

A version of this hymn, changed so as to be an address to the poet, and beginning

Thou, often wandering near
    The stormy river,—

is inscribed over his grave in Trefriw Churchyard, where he lies beside his parents and his wife, under the sombre shadow of ' the twin yew-trees.'

CHAPTER IX.

In some respects the Rev. Dr. William Rees (*Hiraethog*) ranks as the greatest Welshman of the nineteenth century. Preacher and lecturer, journalist and reformer, poet and essayist, there are whole pages in the national history of Wales covered with his broad and sturdy handwriting. But his poetical genius was too massive to produce hymns of the first order. Most of them lack the smoothness of expression and neatness of form so necessary in the making of a good hymn.

One of the gifts of his muse is a new poetical version of the Psalms. How the ministry of affliction helped him to accomplish this undertaking is told in his own words :

'Failing health kept me almost wholly at home during the winter and spring of 1872-3, even as late as the middle of the month of April scarcely venturing out of the house, except on the Sabbath. I consecrated every hour of every day that my weary nature could endure, through the space of the time mentioned, to the task of completing what remained of this work, together with attending to the calls of the pulpit:—and when the clock was striking four, in the afternoon of Friday, March 21, 1873, I was letting the pen out of my hand, having written the last line of the versification. It would not be easy for me to forget how I felt that moment. I gave thanks from my heart, I believe, to the Father of all mercies for having suffered me to live to see this labour completed ; and I tried to dedicate it to the blessing of Him who had supported and strengthened me to carry it through, with a degree of confidence that some might derive benefit and pleasure from its perusal through that blessing. Many a time when, suffering and afflicted, I was at the task, I thought of the words of the Psalmist—" Unless Thy law had been my delights, I should then have perished in mine affliction." So I said :—Had the Psalms not been my delights, I would have perished, from suffering of body and depression of spirit, many a day during that season when I was like Paul, to some extent as it were a prisoner in my own hired house.'

Of the two Psalters of the present century that of Nicander is more marked for smoothness; but that of Hiraethog possesses more originality, and makes a very useful companion of the Psalms in the study.

The hymn-poem of which a version is given below gains an additional interest from the undertone of personal experience easily recognized among the broader movements of a universal theme. Its dramatic cast, however, renders it, like his Psalter, more useful for private devotion than for public worship. It has found its way into most of the later hymn-books of Wales, and is known far and wide.

THE SEARCH OF A TIRED SOUL FOR REST.

I went searching through creation
   For my soul a place of rest—
Disappointment and vexation
   Everywhere repaid my quest.
From the world and flesh to tempt me
   Came a thousand promised joys;
But I found them false and empty,
   Lying dreams and gilded toys.

Then I asked the white and holy
   Angel-thousands of the skies—
' With a sinner poor and lowly
   Have you one will sympathize ? '
Gabriel answered my appealing—
   ' Not with us; no, there is none
That can have a fellow-feeling
   With a soul unclean—undone !

Hope in utter darkness vanished,
   And I cried in agony—
' All deliverance is banished !
   It is over now with me ! '
Stormy clouds on Sinai setting,
   And my spirit trembling sore—
Oh ! there can be no forgetting
   Of that anguish evermore !

On the throne of high possession,
  Through my tears at last I see,
In His robes of intercession,
  Him who bowed the head for me:
'There He is!' my soul exclaimèd,
  'I can read it in His face—
He will never be ashamèd
  To receive me in His grace.'

To His throne my soul proceeded,
  Deigning at His feet to fall;
And for love and pardon pleaded
  Through the blood that saveth all:
'What?'—I mused—'Should I conceal it,
  All this grief and broken cheer?
Hide the wound while He can heal it?
  It is Christ!—why need I fear?'

When I opened, slowly, sadly,
  My dark bosom, sin-oppressed,
Then He opened quickly, gladly,
  For my shelter His own breast:
All my burden He removèd,
  Yea, He gave me full release;
With the smile of my Belovèd
  Came the joy of perfect peace.

Body, spirit, now I owe Him,
  I belong to Him henceforth—
Oh, that I might live to show Him
  Everywhere in all His worth!
When I join the host surrounding
  His serene, eternal throne,
I shall sing of grace abounding,
  And the song shall be His own

The other hymn of his we give has for its
theme Christ weeping over Jerusalem (Luke xix.
28–48).

Lo, He wept! Who, then, is He?
　Christ the Lord! What shall we say?
Thousands wept before; but see
　God as Man in tears to-day.

Lo, He wept! And why should He?
　Oh, not for Himself one tear!
It was human misery
　That had touched His soul so near.

Lo, He wept! And all around
　See the crowd exulting leaps;
Loud and far the songs resound;
　They rejoice—He only weeps.

Lo, He wept! He sees the doom
　Of the city close at hand:
Soon to fall in awful gloom,
　In the fire a burning brand!

Lo, He wept! What love hath He
　For His enemies revealed!
Tears of gentle charity—
　'Tis the heart of God unsealed.

Lo, He wept! Ah, sinner, see—
　See, the tears are falling fast!
He of pity wept for thee—
　And wilt thou not weep at last?

Dr. Rees was born in the month of November, 1802, at the foot of Hiraethog Hill, near Denbigh. It was in the same month, eighty-one years later, that he fell asleep in the city of Chester. 'The search of a tired soul for rest' came to an end, when the Saviour met him at the door and asked him to come in.

A close friend and fellow-worker of the last was the Rev. WILLIAM AMBROSE *Emrys*. He was born at the Penrhyn Arms Hotel, Bangor, August 10, 1813. The course of his life was even and calm as the flowing of a river through a level land, his death alone adding an incident of startling impressiveness to his earthly story. He was preaching in his own pulpit at Portmadoc on Sunday, April 27, 1873. For some time he had been suffering much from the effect of a paralytic stroke; but that was a day of marked power, and the people felt the peculiar nearness of the spirit land. The text of the evening sermon was Isaiah vii. 15 : 'For thus saith the High and Lofty One that inhabiteth eternity, whose name is Holy ; I dwell in the high and the holy place, with him also that is of a contrite and humble spirit, to revive the spirit of the humble, and to revive the heart of the contrite ones.' It was a remarkably powerful sermon ; and hundreds were rejoicing that night in the hope of restored eloquence and further guiding of their soul through him into the doctrine of Jesus Christ. But he had scarcely come down from the pulpit when he was seen to grow pale and lean heavily

Lord, until we reach uphold us!
  It is but a little while ;
When the journey darkly closes
  Let Thy sunlight on us smile :
Let the breezes of the Home-land
  Meet us in the valley's gloom ;
Till our feet are safely treading
  Hills of light and fadeless bloom.

The Rev. WILLIAM THOMAS (*Islwyn*) was born at
Mynydd-islwyn, in the county of Monmouth, April
3, 1832. His life was spent in the secluded and
undisturbed neighbourhood of his birth ; and there
he died November 20, 1878. Purposing in his
early youth to become a land surveyor, at the age
of twenty-two the inward impulse led him to the
pulpit. He was ordained at Llangeitho Association in 1859, but he never took a pastoral charge.
He suffered much from melancholy. In consequence
his preaching engagements were not kept as faithfully as they should have been. Sometimes an elder
would announce him in the following significant
terms : ' Islwyn will preach here next Sunday—if
he comes.'

His poetry stands among the best in Welsh
literature, deeply tinged as it is with the un-
familiar idealizings of a mystic soul. Only three
of his hymns are published. The one given below
has already found a place in the hymnody of the
Welsh Church, and has its record among the songs
ordained of the Holy Spirit to give stay and

patience of hope to the righteous in the hour of
sorrow and death.

See, my soul, the land of brightness
  Far above the clouds of time ;
Where the breeze with balmy lightness
  Bloweth through a genial clime ;
    Joyful thousands !
  Moving in its rest serene.

Life has there its crystal fountains,
  Peace—whose rivers softly flow,
To refresh its vales and mountains,
  To immortalize its glow ;
    And salvation ·
  On the sunny shores is breathed.

Never can a mortal arrow
  On its nearest province fall :
Death's dominion is but narrow—
  There it cometh not at all :
    Life abundant ;
  Immortality at home !

Every breeze of winter changes
  On the shore to heavenly calm ;
O'er its fields no sorrow ranges,
  Every sigh becomes a psalm :
    Into Jordan
  Falls the last most bitter tear.

There—there is not one that mourneth,
  There—there is not any sad ;
There—the gall to honey turneth,
  There—the bound is free and glad :
    Joyful thousands !
  There abiding evermore !

Now my heart is filled with blessing,
  And a sacred joy is mine,
In the hope of soon possessing
  That inheritance Divine :
    Joyful thousands !
  Drawing near that promised land !

CHAPTER X.

S. R.—DAVID JONES OF TREBORTH—ROGER EDWARDS—THOMAS REES, D.D.

THE REV. SAMUEL ROBERTS—better known as S. R. —was born at Llanbrynmair, on the 6th of March, 1800. His father before him was a preacher of high worth, and a father of·many churches; he contributed largely to theological literature, and was a trustee and correspondent of *The Evangelical Magazine*. The son was also an indefatigable worker, and divided his life between America and Wales. He used his pen lavishly on behalf of all reforms, whether in public economy or church principles, whether in social movements or in religious progress. He was an uncompromising iconoclast, and possibly spent too much of his time and talent in 'handling the bow.' He died at Conway in the month of October, 1885.

In 1841 he published a collection of over two thousand hymns, which passed through at least eight editions. It is a very fine collection, and has several hymns and translations by the editor. The names of authors, however, are not given.

I must therefore give the following selections as anonymous:

THE FRUITS OF CHRIST'S TRAVAIL.

Our dearest Lord went forth to sow in tears,
   When days were dark, when He was weary too;
But now the joy of harvest-tide appears,
   And for His toil shall endless praise be due.

As firstfruits went He to the blessed land,
   And from His woe shall fields of harvest rise;
It shall be gathered by the Lord's own hand,
   From earth's four corners to th' eternal skies.

MINISTERING ANGELS.

Great God, to what glory and lofty estate
Thine Only-begotten was raised, and made great!
The angels in dazzling white garments are known
As ministers of His untarnishèd throne.

The angels are bidden to guide us who roam,
To lead us and bring us the narrow way home;
Whatever the dangers that crowd on the road,
They meet us in journeying homeward to God.

When I must depart from this frail tent of dust,
When I must appear at the throne of the Just,
Oh, let a kind angel from Paradise come,
To guide and defend me and bring me safe home.

What of the Night?

Watchman, say, what of the night?
  Is the dawning still afar?
Pilgrim, see, so fair and bright,
  O'er the hills the Morning-Star:
Watchman, what denotes its sign?
  Is it better time for man?
Pilgrim, 'tis the dawn Divine
  Of the everlasting plan.

Watchman, say, what of the night?
  Is it still not nearing day?
Pilgrim, night is done! the light
  Spreads upon its glorious way:
Watchman, why departest thou?
  Why turn home when all is gain?
Pilgrim, o'er the wide earth now
  Comes the Prince of Peace to reign!

The Marriage of the Lamb.[1]

I.

Who the Prince?—and what the chariot
  O'er the starry pathways led?
Armies follow on white horses,
  Many crowns are on His head:
    King of glory!
  On His robe the name is read.

---

[1] These verses are by Rev. John Roberts, Llangwm.

9

His look pierceth through creation,
  Flames within His eyes abide :
Who is this—but Zion's Bridegroom ?
  Gently smiles He on His bride :
    His the garment
With His life-blood deeply dyed.

II.

Who is this fair Bride approaching
  Through the gates of death serene ?
Lo, the beauteous light of dawning
  Blushing leaves the radiant scene :
    She is Zion,
In fine linen white and clean.

Through the shining realms of starlight
  Let the angels clear the way ;
Let all Nature wear its glory,
  And each flower its sweet array :
    Sing the marriage
Of the Lamb in many a lay.

THE LORD'S TABLE.

The table of Thy grace,
  Lord, here I take my place ;
Let me Thy face behold well pleased :
  Thy face, my dearest Lord,
  Doth highest joy afford,
And love's sweet word lights up the feast.

When musing I draw near
The woe of nail and spear,
With reverent fear my spirit guide :
Let me Thy freedom share,
Make strong my faith to bear
Thine ark with care till eventide.

Soon, soon doth time remove
These earthly feasts of love—
The sorrow of the world remains :
But in that sweet countrie
No sword to bear have we,
For charity unending reigns.

The Rev. DAVID JONES (of Treborth) was born June 2, 1805, in the parish of Dolyddelen, Caernarvonshire. His eldest brother was the celebrated Welsh preacher—John Jones, Talysarn. Neither of them as children had any opportunities of education beyond what the Sunday - school provided. Their father died when the eldest brother was only ten and the youngest only two. So, as they grew up, the former went to work in the slate quarry, and the latter stayed at home to work on the farm for his mother. David Jones, from his boyhood, was fond of preaching: often he would retire to some unfrequented spot and become both preacher and audience himself. He was twenty - one years old when he gave his first sermon in public, and soon came into note. He, like his brother, had the true instinct of self-culture, which saved

him to a large extent from the misfortune of
early disadvantages. He was ordained at Bala
in 1834, and laboured successively at Caernarvon, Treborth, and Llanfairfechan, where he died
June 23, 1868. He published three extensive
poems on the subjects of ' The Prodigal Son,'
' Christ's Sacrifice,' and ' Man.' The spirit of his
poetry is well represented by such verses as these :

> The Sacrifice wickedly slain
>   On Calvary one afternoon,
> Did God for atonement ordain,
>   And He is well pleased in the Son :
> His merit no language can tell,
>   The title of Godhead is His ;
> No praises can ever excel
>   The worth of a Saviour like this.
>
> The earth is so little, beside
>   Creation's unmeasurèd reach—
> A small speck of dust undescried,
>   A drop of the sea on the beach :
> But Love wrought its victory here,
>   A conquest of glory supreme ;
> And Calvary's accent is clear
>   Through heaven in each rapturous theme.
>
> Awake ! it is time, oh ! my soul,
>   Be strong to forget every pain ;
> The Church of all nations extol,
>   The praise of the Lamb that was slain :
> The work is so vast in its plan,
>   Too few are the words of the earth,
> Too feeble the talents of man,
>   To tell the Atonement's full worth.

The Feast of Atonement is nigh,
  The world is to share in the feast—
Let all the bright stars of the sky
  Be bells of fine gold for the Priest!
His praise let all powers make known—
  ' He reconciled us unto God!
The Aaron who died to atone,
  He liveth, with glory endowed.'

Let all worlds in concert unite
  To give the Redeemer His due,
Until their rejoicing delight
  Th' eternal dominions of blue:
All space be an ocean of praise,
  And waves of harmonious refrain
Surge back over infinite ways
  To the shores of creation again!

Oh! sinner, hast thou not a voice
  For Him who is Refuge alone!
The angels adoring rejoice
  That He for us all did atone:
Their wonder they ever confess,
  To think of His death in our room:
But is their astonishment less,
  That man should keep silent and dumb?

Awake! to the Lamb be thy song!
  Whose debt can be ever so great?
In singing His praises grow strong;
  Begin,—'tis already so late!
The song of the white-wingèd quire
  Is weak for that triumph of love:
Stand thou in thy part, and aspire
  To add to the rapture above.

The angels in singing proclaim,
‘Christ Jesus! our Wonder is He : ’
But man has much more in the Name—
‘Christ Jesus is Life unto me ! ’
They wonder to think of Him dead—
For thee did He journey that way :
The angels can call Him their Head—
‘My Brother’ canst thou to Him say ?

The Rev. ROGER EDWARDS was born January 22, 1811, at Bala—a name associated for ever with some of the noblest and most romantic traditions of Methodist piety. He received a good education, and preached his first sermon on the verge of his twentieth year. In the year 1834 he settled at Mold, and there he remained till the end of his days. No one ever deserved a title better than he did that of ‘Bishop of Flintshire,’ given him by the unanimous voice of the people. His memory remains beloved in all the Churches. Possibly, however, in after years his name will be remembered more through his intimate connection with the rise of Welsh periodical literature. He settled at Mold for the purpose of editing one of the pioneer newspapers of the Principality. In 1846 he was appointed sole editor of *Y Drysorfa*, the monthly organ of the Calvinistic Methodists; and he held the appointment until his death. But perhaps still more important was his connection with the premier review of Wales—*Y Traethodydd*—started, in 1845, under the joint-editorship of himself and the late

Dr. Edwards, of Bala. In 1840 he edited a de-
nominational hymn-book, for which he wrote
several hymns. He also published, in 1855, a
volume of moral and sacred songs, which has
passed into a second edition. Simple, chaste,
and serious is the note of all he did. The first
given is a song of early piety:

Dear is the advent of the spring,
  With sunny smiles aglow;
When Nature leaves her languishing,
  And all things beauteous grow.

Dear is the face of early rose
  Where'er it first appears;
How fair its purple mantle shows,
  Softened with dewy tears!

Dear is the plant that yields its spoil
  The first of all the rest;
It pays for all the anxious toil,
  And care itself is blest.

Dear is the innocent delight
  Of lamb in gleesome play;
And sweet to hear the birds unite
  In song at break of day.

But only some frail shadowing
  Is all on earth we see;
Dearer than every joy of spring
  Is early piety.

Oh! scene most fair—some glad young heart
    Walking with Christ in light;
Thus earth and heaven take a part
    In witnessing the sight.

The zeal that works with quiet rule,
    Bright looks, affections warm,
Make him in God's work beautiful,
    As morning's pleasant charm.

True piety in early days
    Its joy through life supplies;
It brings its heir through all rough ways
    To live in Paradise.

The next is a favourite Christmas hymn:

What is in Ephrata heard?
Angels bringing joyful word:
What new song of heaven have they?
Christ is born! is born to-day!
Haste to David's city, haste!
God is there made manifest;
See the King of glory, see,
Brother of us all is He!

Silent babe, what name has He?
Lord of all eternity:
What hath brought Him down so low?
Love for sinful man to show:—
Wings of tender mercies bright
Brought Him down from heaven's height;
Let the beauty of His praise
Ever be on all our days.

To the angels what is He?
Their high Prince of majesty;
What to us who sin and fall?
He is Brother of us all:
Then if angel-harps be His,
What we owe much larger is:
Christ the Lord—He is our own!
Let the wide earth be His throne.

The author of the *History of Protestant Non-conformity in Wales* is by no means an unknown name in England. The Rev. Dr. REES, of Swansea, was an interpreter of Welsh religious movements to his English brethren. He anxiously watched the growth of English speech in South Wales, and the large inflow of English people; he also saw how urgent it became to meet the new conditions. So he kept pleading for sympathy and help in a work that may well be called missionary; and he had the satisfaction of seeing his pleadings honoured, and a great movement inaugurated. He was born December 13, 1815, in the parish of Llanfynydd, Caermarthenshire, amid circumstances poor enough. His school-days were limited to one quarter; but, luckily—like many others who have become princes of the Welsh pulpit—he knew how to be his own teacher. As a boy he was put down as good-for-nothing; but the moment he found entrance into the pulpit his life-work was begun. He was abundant in labour, whether for the pulpit or for the press. He translated the commentary

of Albert Barnes on the New Testament into Welsh;
and in his latter years he published an edition of
the Bible with devotional annotations. In 1884 he
was elected chairman of the Congregational Union
of England and Wales—the first Welsh minister to
be so honoured. And his chairmanship was to be
honoured of heaven; for a few days before the May
meetings of 1885 had come he lay at rest. His
address was ready, on ' The Power of the Pulpit ; '
but on the 29th of April God called him to join
the congregation of the first-born, leaving the
vacant chair for another to fill. He is doubly
deserving of a place here—both for the hymns he
wrote and for the affectionate care with which he
has saved the scant history of several hymn-writers
from being utterly forgotten. Several of his hymns
were meant for harvest thanksgivings; and one of
these is given below :

Let us thank the Lord together
　For the mercies of His hand ;
Once again the crown of plenty
　Blesses all this happy land :
Gracious are the Father's ways,
Let us bring Him comely praise.

Though our faults have cried in heaven
　For His vengeance on our head,
Yet hath He preserved unbroken
　For our good the staff of bread :
God of patience is He named,
Loud His praises be proclaimed !

Give us grace, Lord, in receiving
  Bounteous gifts of Thy left hand,
Lest we may forget the riches
  Of another, better land :
May each precious soul be fed
With the true and living Bread !

The truth of the following hymn is well illus-
trated in the author's own life, remembering his
lowly beginning and the honoured end :

A pilgrim to the pleasant Land,
  Oft hindered on the way,
I keep the path and trust my God—
  For strength comes with the day.

Often have foes beset my soul,
  Which would my faith betray ;
But they have failed to lay me low—
  For strength came with the day.

And should worse enemies arise
  In pitiless array,
My way is forward, fearing nought—
  For strength comes with the day.

When Death, the king of terrors, comes,
  To break my tent of clay,
I shall not fear his ruthless arm—
  For strength comes with the day.

When I shall stand on Canaan's hills,
  In freedom's perfect way,
How sweet will be the joy of praise
  For strength with every day !

CHAPTER XI.

WHERE the whole range of hymnody is so largely picturesque, it may seem superfluous to mark any hymns in particular as pictures. But there are Welsh verses—many of them not found in the ordinary hymn-book—which are so popular, that it would be unfair to leave them unmentioned. They are folk-songs—more often recited than sung. Some striking picture or pretty conceit has appealed successfully to public favour, and passes down from generation to generation, the name of the author being either lost or doubtful.

The late Rev. Paxton Hood has made the name and style of CHRISTMAS EVANS familiar to English readers. He allowed his fancy free range in allegory; and this verse admirably represents the boldness of his style :

On Calvary together
  Two flames were seen to shine ;
A flame of love for sinners,
  A flame of wrath Divine :

Their smoke on high ascended,
  And hid the stars of light;—
Between the two flames, dying,
  Was Jesus—wondrous sight!

The author of the next verse was the Rev.
David Davies, Ebenezer, Swansea:

Golgotha! the greatest battle
  Ever fought was on its height;
There the Lamb without a weapon
  Crushed the dragons in His might:
There He thirsted, there He languished,
  Overcoming hell's despite;
Yet within His heart a fountain
  That can wash the Ethiop white.

Anonymous are the two following verses, given
as examples of the poetry of quaint conceits—
after the manner much affected by such writers
as Herrick, and Crashaw, and George Herbert.
The first is a conceit on Christ as the Rock:

Come and see! A Rock appears,
Bound by men with swords and spears:
Come and see! Alone and still
Hangs a Rock upon the hill:
In a rock a Rock is laid,
Till three days their course have made:
Spite of stone and soldiery,
From the rock a Rock breaks free.

The second is a conceit on Christ as the Sun :

> In sight of the sun was stricken
>   The Sun on Calvary's height ;
> The Sun made the sun to darken—
>   Was it not a wondrous sight ?
> The Sun without sun was buried,
>   And lay in the silent tomb,
> Till the two suns rose together,
>   When the third day's dawn was come.

The author of the next verse is the Rev. Thomas Williams, Bethesda'r Fro, already referred to :

> May He who once at midday
>   Sat down by Jacob's well,
> In passing through Samaria—
>   Now come with us to dwell :
> Athirst to save the people
>   Was Jesus Christ of yore ;
> Athirst is He in heaven
>   To save yet many more.

The name of Dr. PHILLIPS, Neuaddlwyd, can never be separated from the history of religion in Wales during the first half of the present century. He was a pioneer of education—especially in the training of young men for the ministry. It was pre-eminently a labour of love ; his influence therefore on his pupils, and through them on the churches, was immense. He was an enthusiast of foreign missions, and had the pleasure of ordaining three young men out of his own Church as missionaries. He was born in the parish of Llanvihangel-ar-Arth, Caermarthenshire, March 29, 1772, and died December 2, 1842. A few single verses of his are very popular—none more so than the one translated thus:

> Once again the world shall see
> Him who went to Calvary,
> Sitting throned in high command,
> With the balance in His hand:
> All of every time and place
> Shall be weighed before His face:
> Seek, my soul, the pearl most rare,
> That will turn the balance there!

The River of Death—a favourite picture of every Welsh hymn-writer—is the theme of the next verse:

> I must cross a mighty river,
>   Deep between two worlds it flows;
> And the sounding of its waters
>   Are these many earthly woes:
> In its waves in sorest anguish
>   I shall very soon be found—
> Oh! for Christ as my foundation!
>   Then my feet shall touch the ground.

A variation on the same theme is the following:

Seek thou, my soul, in earnest,
　　The Rock to build upon,
The only place of resting,
　　The sure foundation-stone:
How sweet within the river
　　The Rock that will not fail,
When every storm is breaking
　　This soul of mine so frail.

The author of the latter was the Rev. TITUS
LEWIS, a celebrated Baptist minister. He was
born at Cilgerran, Pembrokeshire, Feb. 21, 1774,
and died at Caermarthen, May 1, 1811. He was
a contemporary and co-worker with Christmas
Evans, and he spent his brief life in unwearied
labours for the pulpit and for native literature.
He had very few advantages of early education,
and yet he wrote a *Political and Religious History
of Great Britain*, he published a Welsh-English
Dictionary, and had most to do with translating
Dr. Gill's commentary into Welsh, as well as several
other works.

Another variation on the same theme is from the
pen of the Rev. JOHN ROBERTS, Conway—a brother
of S. R., and better known also by his initials as
J. R.:

A weary traveller
　　Beside the River stood;
His lamp was in his hand,
　　And shone across the flood:
It brought the other shore in sight,
Where many angels walked in white.

10

In fear he took his steps
   Down to the water's brim;
But through the darkness vast
   Clear shone the lamp for him:
And through the surge the angels bright
Can see him coming in its light.

Behold, his great High Priest
   Among the shining throng!
And He is coming down
   To break the current strong:
The land in safety he hath won,
That needs not any lamp or sun.

S. R. himself is the author of this song:

Afar on the ocean, one dark and cold night,
A little boat sailed without star or moon-light;
The roar of the wind and the rush of the wave
That night even frightened the heart of the brave

The child of the captain was free from alarm,
All happy and merry he dreaded no harm:—
'In spite of the wild waves what is there to fear?
We are sure to reach home —*for my father doth
steer.*'

Oh, dear child of heaven, what makes thee afraid?
When high seas are raging be thou not dismayed
When wildest and blackest the great depths appear,
Thy life is still safe—*for thy Father doth steer.*

Rejoicing eternal for thee is at hand ;
Thy loved ones are waiting on yonder fair strand :
Thy home is the mansion that shineth so clear,
And Canaan is nearing—*thy Father doth steer.*

Then spread forth thy sails to the favouring breeze,
The bosom of Jesus will soon give thee ease :
Thine anchor is safe, and thy Captain is here,
Thy boat's in the haven—*thy Father doth steer.*

To close this chapter of pictures and conceits, we give this spiritual romance in miniature, from the pen of a living writer—Mr. WILLIAM JONES (*Ehedydd Ial*), Llandegla :

The sky became at noon
    As black as very night ;
With neither sun nor moon,
    Nor any star of light :
And from the cloud stern Justice hurled
Its lightning through the darkened world.

With guilty fears beset,
    My conscience cried dismayed ;
And ne'er shall I forget
    That bitter cry for aid :
In agony I turned and fled,
Not knowing where to hide my head.

I reached the Law's strait door,
    Hoping to find release ;
I pleaded, faint and sore,
    For refuge and for peace :
' Flee for thy life,' she said, ' from me,
To the Son of Man on Calvary ! '

Fleeing, I tried to flee,
  Amid the thunders' roar ;
The lightning followed me,
  Like some red host of war :
I came at last to Calvary—
There Jesus only could I see.

What though my flesh be grass,
  And all my bones but clay,
I'll sing where lightnings pass—
  'God took my sins away !'
The Rock of Ages—there I've stood :
Quenched are the lightnings in His blood !

CHAPTER XII.

VERSES WITH A HISTORY.

No story of the Welsh hymns would be complete
without a note on the influence of single verses.
The hymn-book in the pew is an innovation—quite
within recent years—of Welsh church-life.   The
hymn-book used to be the private property of the
pulpit; consequently the people had to learn their
favourite hymns by heart—and a very profitable
exercise it always is.   A hymn within the heart is
life.   But in learning hymns it often happens that
one special verse stands out from among its sister
verses.   The latter may be forgotten; the one
clings to the memory.   This single verse of
Williams, Pantycelyn, has been the password of
many a powerful revival, the last two lines being
doubled and trebled over and over again, as the
hearts of the congregation were moved by the
breath from Calvary :

> Jesu's blood can raise the feeble
> As a conqueror to stand ;
> Jesu's blood is all-prevailing
> O'er the mighty of the land :
> Let the breezes
> Blow from Calvary on me.

Another verse, vividly associated with times of refreshing, is the following by Morgan Rhys :

> Thy gracious ancient promise
> Has saved a countless host,
> Who sing its praise for ever—
> Once they were of the lost :
> Though often sorely wounded
> With evil in the strife,
> They found the leaves of healing
> Upon the tree of life.

It is an old funeral custom in country districts of the Principality to sing on the road from the house to the churchyard. The funerals are mostly public, and there is generally a large concourse of people. The procession moves slowly on, singing here and there, as it moves, some measured, mournful melody, with a wondrously touching effect. If any one has ever heard this music of the dead coming with muffled far-off tones from some narrow, lonely glen, he will never forget it. It is a minor melody that is sung, whether the words be of sorrow or of hope. Among the verses I have often heard on these occasions is this, by Thomas Williams :

> Oh ! what distances eternal
> Are to-day before my face ;
> Never staying, never resting,
> I must journey to my place :
> Though so narrow,
> I must through the gateway pass.

And this other, by Williams, Pantycelyn:

> When human help is at an end,
>   God's pity shall not languish;
> He will be Father, Brother, Friend,
>   In death's relentless anguish.

But no verse has so hallowed the presence of death as the following, the author of which seems to be unknown:

> There shall be thousand wonders,
>   At break of day, to see
> The children of the tempests
>   From tribulation free;
> All in their snow-white garments,
>   In new and perfect guise,
> Upon their Saviour's likeness,
>   Out of the grave they rise.[1]

---

[1] This verse having been of late rather prominently brought before the English public, through its being sung at the London National Eisteddvod and beside the grave of the late Henry Richard, M.P., several attempts have been made to translate it. Below is a rendering by Mr. Josiah D. Evans (*Ap Daniel*), New York:

> Ten thousand glorious wonders
>   Shall greet the morning ray;
> When earth's storm-beaten children
>   Shall wake to endless day;
> All clad in robes of whiteness,
>   And crowned with fadeless bloom;
> In their Redeemer's likeness,
>   Ascending from the tomb!

Sung to a tune of its own, the impressiveness of
the verse in the original is most profound. Every
separate line—almost every word—seems to have
a history. However neatly translated, this history
is always wanting in the new language. Hence
the translator's despair.

Perhaps no single verse in Welsh hymnody has
such a romantic incident in its history as the one
given below, written, as it was, by Williams on
the occasion of the memorable Lisbon earthquake:

> If Thou would'st end the world, O Lord,
> Accomplish first Thy promised word,
> And gather home with one accord
>   From every part Thine own :
> Send out Thy word from pole to pole,
> And with Thy blood make thousands whole,
> Till health has come to every soul,
>   And after that—come down !

In February, 1797, the French effected a landing
near Fishguard, in Pembrokeshire. Napoleon was
then a name of terror to England ; and the news
of the landing spread through the country with
the rushing violence of a prairie fire, bringing
with it wherever it went an overwhelming sense
of doom. Mounted heralds posted through the
length and breadth of Wales, without waiting to
ascertain the force of the enemy. In every village
and town the terrible message was left, and people
generally made ready for the bitter end of all

things. One of these fiery heralds happened to pass by the Independent Chapel at Rhydybont, Cardiganshire, where a preaching service was being held at the time. Mysteriously he whispered his wild message to some one near the door, and away he went again to scatter broadcast the seeds of a storm. From one to another in the chapel the news mysteriously flashed—the curiosity of those who did not know being almost as tragic as the consternation of those who knew. The preacher was confounded, and he was compelled to stop and ask for the cause of such unseemly commotion. Some one shouted—' The French have landed at Fishguard!' Bad before, it was worse now. Had a lightning struck the house, the panic could scarcely have been more overpowering. No one durst move or speak; the preacher himself sat down in the midst of his sermon utterly overborne. Only one soul was found equal to the occasion—and that a woman's soul. Let the name of Nancy Jones not be forgotten in the chronicles of noble women who have dared and endured. She never for a moment slackened her hold of the Higher Will. She was a true daughter of the Great Revival: a neighbour, too, of David Jones, of Cayo. At many a service before that day her voice had been sweetest and fullest in the fervour of song. She called to the preacher when he stopped—' Go on: if the French are at Fishguard, we have God to take care of us.' But the preacher still declined. A

neighbour of hers—David John Edmund by name
—was present, remarkable for his gift in prayer.
To him she turned next, and asked him to pray.
But even he was not one of five that could chase
a hundred that day. 'Well, then,' she said,
'give a verse out for us to sing.' No; David John
had no heart for so much as that. 'Very well,'
this mother in Israel added, 'I shall give out a
verse myself, and you start the tune.' Calm and
solemn and sweet echoed the words through the
building—

If Thou would'st end the world, O Lord,

and so on to the end of the verse. Great was the
fall of David John; even his tunes had taken
unto themselves wings. She had to start the tune
herself; but scarcely had she struck the first notes
before her courage with an electric thrill restored
the congregation to spiritual consciousness. They
joined in the song of their new Deborah; faith
grew more steady and clear; the French were
well-nigh forgotten in the glorious inspiration of
'the promised word.' A woman's faith has often
in it something of a miracle.

CHAPTER XIII.

HYMNS OF TO-DAY.

For all the hymns which have been written, there is room in the Wales of to-day for a new school of hymnody. Every age has its peculiar mode of religious expression; the age now dawning in Wales emphatically so. It will be an age of transition and suspense; it will claim the guidance of strong, progressive thought. I trust the Eisteddvod will not exhaust the muse of all its bards. Some of them, surely, will not consider it a vain thing to give the Church of Christ the psalm that will sanctify its anxiety, that will teach it where to find rest and hope and light.

It will not be amiss, therefore, to close the present volume with a few gleanings from contemporary poetry.

The first is from the pen of a preacher as well known almost in England as he is in Wales— the Rev. Dr. Herber Evans, of Caernarvon:

> Keep me very near to Jesus,
>   Though beneath His cross it be;
> In this world of evil-doing
>   'Tis the cross that cleanseth me:

Should there come distress and darkness,
   Let this hope with me abide—
After all the gloom and sorrow,
   Light shall be at eventide.

Bring to mind my past experience—
   That shall take my fears away;
For Thy goodness and Thy mercy
   Shall be mine till close of day:
Through the tears, the clouds, the tempest,
   Shine on me, O Crucified!
There's a promise in God's rainbow—
   Light shall be at eventide.

Lead me onward to the future,
   Where I fear one step to move;
Still the love of God will keep me—
   Love beyond a mother's love:
Calvary has said sufficient—
   Hear them sing on yonder side:
Though the cross stand in the pathway,
   Light shall be at eventide.

The Rev. THOMAS LEVI, Aberystwith, through his popular children's monthly—*Trysorfa y Plant*—has been for years a close friend of the children of the Principality: and among other things he has written several charming hymns for their use. The following is one of his:

The ark upon the deluge
   Was Noah's safe abode;
Though sail and helm were wanting,
   His Captain then was God:

The Lord was very angry,
  And all the world was drowned:
Not even lofty mountains
  Could anywhere be found.
    Though sail and helm be wanting,
      If the ark be our abode,
    We'll sing above the deluge—
      Our Captain still is God!

Eight souls alone were rescued
  To walk the earth again—
Through them a thousand counsels
  Wrought out the good of men:
The Babe adored of shepherds
  In little Bethlehem,
And Calvary's great Passion—
  All came of saving them.

The Lord of Hosts remembered
  His covenant of peace;
And He remembered Noah,
  And made the waters cease:
A gracious sign He granted,
  His faithfulness to prove—
The tender leaf of olive
  Brought by the white-winged dove.
    Though sail and helm be wanting,
      If the ark be our abode,
    We'll sing above the deluge—
      Our Captain still is God!

The next two are by well-known bards of the
Eisteddvod,—the first by the Rev. EVAN REES
(*Dyfed*):

Calvary, with radiance glowing,
  Thither now I turn my face;
Immortality is flowing
  From above in streams of grace:
    'Heights of Calvary!'
Build thy nest there, O my soul!

There I hear in breezes mellow
  Sounds from far of heavenly themes,
Learnt of yore beneath the willow
  On the bank of Babel's streams:
    'Heights of Calvary'
Join the earth to heaven's land.

Scorchèd in the flame of burning,
  See the thief's uncared-for soul,
At the last to heaven turning,
  Pitied—rescued—and made whole:
    'Heights of Calvary'
Shall his song for ever be.

In the vale with shadows crowded,
  When I sink with sore dismay,
Calvary will stand unclouded
  In its baptism of day:
    'Heights of Calvary'
Are transfigured by the cross.

Once its summit was benighted
  With a cloud of wrath Divine,
But Atonement's sun has lighted
  All the hill as mercy's shrine:
    'Heights of Calvary!'
Never more shall night come there.

Oh, to climb in holy fancies,
  On my knees, this Mount of love !
There I see, through tearful glances,
  Nothing save the cross above :
    'Heights of Calvary'
Make my tears a stream of peace !

'Heights of Calvary' (*Pen Calfaria*)—it should be noted—is a well-known refrain in a revival verse of Williams.

The closing hymn of the book is by Mr. BENJAMIN DAVIES (*T'afolog*). 'Unto Him' (*Iddo Ef*) has become a separate phrase in the language of Welsh devotion :

Through the eternal blue
The circling worlds renew
  Their joyful hymn :
They sing in mighty chord,
Like mountain floods outpoured—
'Not unto us, O Lord,
  But—Unto Him ! '

Great winds and waves unite
With thunders to recite
  The choral theme :
The pleasant whispering rill,
The voice of torrent shrill,
The storm from hill to hill,
  Sing—'Unto Him ! '

The wingcd quircs of Spring
Make all the woodlands ring
    With grateful hymn :
Each leafy bush ablaze
Its altar doth upraise,
For festivals of praise
    Held ' unto Him.'

Soul ! would'st thou turn aside
This praise to thine own pride,
    Making it dim ?
The song of self in thee
Would break the harmony
Which floweth full and free,
    All—' Unto Him.'

Like some frail shower-drop,
Losing itself in hope
    To find the sea,—
Let charity's sweet reign
Grant me the sacred gain,
To lose, and still retain
    Myself in Thee.

Myself no more I know
By Jesu's cup of woe,
    Filled to the brim :
Dying beside God's rood,
Beneath the tears and blood,
Is life's beatitude,
    Sealed ' unto Him.'

If Jesus sowed in tears
The harvest of the years,
    When days were dim;
One day shall stand revealed
His golden harvest-field,
And all the worlds shall yield,
    Praise—unto Him.

INDEX.